BOUND BY A BABY

BOUND BY A BABY

BY

KATE HARDY

Published in Great Britain 2013
by Mills & Boon, an imprint of Harlequin (UK) Limited.
Large Print edition 2014
Harlequin (UK) Limited, Eton House,
18-24 Paradise Road, Richmond, Surrey, TW9 1SR

© 2013 Pamela Brooks

ISBN: 978 0 263 24011 5

Printed and bound in Great Britain
by CPI Antony Rowe, Chippenham, Wiltshire

For Gerard, Chris and Chloe—
the best research team ever—with all my love.

CHAPTER ONE

'I ASSUME YOU know why you're both here,' the solicitor said, looking at Emmy and then at Dylan.

Of course Emmy knew. Ally and Pete had asked her to be their son Tyler's guardian, if the unthinkable should ever happen.

If. She swallowed hard. That was the whole point of her being here. Because the unthinkable *had* happened. And Emmy still couldn't quite believe that she'd never see her best friend again.

She lifted her chin. Obviously today was about making things all official legally. And as for Dylan Harper—the only man she'd ever met who could make wearing a T-shirt and jeans feel as if they were a formal business suit—he was obviously here because he was Pete's best friend and Pete and Ally had asked him to be the executor of their will. 'Yes,' she said.

'Yes,' Dylan echoed.

'Good.' The solicitor tapped his pen against his blotter. 'So, Miss Jacobs, Mr Harper, can you confirm that you're both prepared to be Tyler's guardians?'

Emmy froze for a moment. *Both?* What was the man talking about? No way would Ally and Pete have asked them both to be Tyler's guardian. There had to be some mistake.

She glanced at Dylan, to find him looking straight back at her. And his expression was just as stunned as her own must be.

Or maybe they'd misheard. Misunderstood. 'Both of us, Tyler's guardians?' she asked.

For the first time, the solicitor's face showed an expression other than smooth neutrality. 'Did you not know they'd named you as Tyler's guardian in the will, Ms Jacobs?'

Emmy blew out a breath. 'Well, yes. Ally asked me before she and Pete revised their wills.' And she'd assumed that Ally had meant *just* her.

'Pete asked me,' Dylan said.

Which almost made Emmy wonder if Ally and Pete hadn't spoken to each other about it. Though obviously they must've done. They'd both signed the will, so they'd clearly known that both of their best friends had agreed to be there for Tyler. They just hadn't shared that particular piece of information with either Dylan or herself, by the looks of things.

'Is there a problem?' the solicitor asked.

Apart from the fact that she and Dylan disliked each other intensely and usually avoided each other? Or the fact that Dylan was married—and Emmy was pretty sure that his wife couldn't be too pleased that her husband had been named co-guardian with another woman, one who was single? 'No,' she said quickly, and looked at Dylan. This was his cue to explain that no, he couldn't do it.

'No problem,' Dylan confirmed, to her shock.

'Good.'

Good? No, it just made everything much more complicated, Emmy thought. Or maybe it meant he intended to fight her for custody of the baby: family man versus single mum, so it was obvious who'd win. But she didn't have a chance to protest because the solicitor went on with the reading of the will. 'Now, obviously Ally and Pete left financial provisions for Tyler. I have all the details here.'

'I'll deal with it,' Dylan said.

Immediately assuming that a flaky, air-headed jewellery designer wouldn't have a clue what to do? Emmy knew that was how Dylan saw her—she'd overheard him say it to Pete, on more than one occasion—and it rankled. She'd been her own boss for ten years. She was perfectly capable of dealing with things. Whereas he was so uptight and stuffy, she couldn't even begin to imagine him looking after a baby or a toddler. Given that Ally had always been diplomatic about Dylan's wife, merely saying that she worked with Pete, Emmy was pretty sure that Nadine Harper was from the same mould as Dylan. A cold workaholic who wouldn't know what fun was if it jumped out in front of him and yelled, 'Boo!' And not the sort that Ally would've wanted caring for her son.

But the solicitor was off again, going through the details of the arrangements made in the will. Emmy had to ignore her feelings and listen to what the man was telling her before she got completely lost. This was *important*.

And then at last it was all over.

Leaving her and Dylan to pick up the pieces. Together. Unthinkably.

She gave the solicitor a polite smile, shook his hand, and walked out of the office. On the doorstep of the building, she came to a halt and faced Dylan.

'I think,' she said, 'we need to talk. Like *now.*'

He nodded. 'And I could do with some coffee.'

There were shadows under his cornflower-blue eyes, and lines at the corners betraying that he hadn't slept properly since the crash; for the first time ever, Dylan actually looked vulnerable—and as if he hurt as much as she did, right now. It stopped her from uttering the kind of snippy remarks they usually made to each other.

'Make that two of us,' she said. On the sleep front, as well as the need for coffee. Vulnerability, no way would she admit to. Especially not to Dylan Harper. No way was she giving him an excuse to take Tyler from her. He and Nadine were *not* taking her place.

'Where's Tyler?' Dylan asked.

'With my mum. She'll ring me if there's a problem.' She lifted one shoulder, daring him to criticise her. 'I didn't think the solicitor's office would be the best place for him.'

'It isn't.'

Another first: he was actually agreeing with her. Maybe, she thought, they might be able to work something out between them? Maybe he'd be reasonable? A baby wouldn't fit into his busy, workaholic lifestyle. It'd be tough for Emmy, too, but at least she'd spent time with her godson and would have some clue about looking after him.

'Shall we?' she asked, indicating the café across the road.

'Fine.'

At the counter in the café, Emmy ordered a latte. 'What would you like?'

'I'll get these,' Dylan said immediately.

She gave a small but determined shake of her head. No way was she going to let him take charge. 'I offered first.'

'Then thank you—an espresso would be great.'

'Do you want anything to eat?'

He grimaced. 'Thank you for the offer, but right now I really can't face anything.'

She, too, hadn't been able to choke much down

since she'd heard the news. It seemed that the situation had shaken him as much as it had shaken her. In a way, that was a good thing. Maybe they could find some common ground.

'If you go and find us a table, I'll bring our coffee over,' she said.

And she was glad of that small space between them. Just so she could marshal her thoughts. Right now, she didn't want to fight with Dylan. She just wanted her best friend back. For everything to be the same as it had been, three days ago. For Pete to have taken Ally on a surprise anniversary trip to Venice, for them to be happy and for Ally to be texting her to let her know they were on their way back and couldn't wait to see their little boy and tell her all about the trip. For them to be *alive*.

Emmy paid for the coffees, and carried them over to the quiet table Dylan had found for them in the corner.

'So you had no idea Pete had asked me to be Tyler's guardian?' Dylan asked.

Typical Dylan: straight in there. No pussyfooting around. Though, for once, she agreed with him. They needed to cut to the chase. 'No. And you had no idea that Ally had asked me?'

'No.' He spread his hands. 'Of course I said yes when he asked me—just as you obviously did when Ally asked you.' He sighed. 'I know you shouldn't speak ill of the dead—and Pete was my best friend, the closest I had to a brother—but what the *hell* were they thinking when they decided this?'

'They're both—*were* both,' she corrected herself, wincing, 'only children. Pete's dad is nearly eighty and Ally's mum isn't well. How could Pete and Ally's parents be expected to cope with looking after a baby full-time? And it isn't going to get any easier for them over the next twenty years. Of course Pete and Ally would ask someone nearer their own age to be Tyler's guardian.'

Dylan gave a pained sigh. 'I didn't mean *that*. It's obvious. I mean, why *us*?'

Why ask two people who really didn't get on to take care of the most precious thing in their lives? Good question. Though that wasn't the one uppermost in her mind. 'Why you and me instead of you and your wife?' she asked pointedly.

He blew out a breath. 'That isn't an issue.'

'If I was married and my husband's best friend asked him to be the baby's guardian if the worst happened, I'd be pretty upset if another woman was named as the co-guardian instead of me,' Emmy said.

'It isn't an issue,' Dylan repeated.

Patronising, pompous idiot. Emmy kept a rein on her temper. Just. 'Don't you think this discussion ought to include her?'

'You're the one who said we needed to talk.'

'We do.' She switched into superpolite mode, the one she used for difficult clients, before she was tempted to strangle him. 'Could you perhaps phone her and see when's a good time for her to join us?'

'No,' he said tightly.

Superpolite mode off. 'Either she really, *really* trusts you,' Emmy said, 'or you're even more of a control freak than I thought.'

'It isn't an issue,' Dylan said, 'because we're separated.' He glared at her. 'Happy, now?'

What? Since when had Dylan split up with his wife? And why? But Emmy damped the questions down. It wasn't any of her business.

Whereas Tyler's welfare—that was most definitely her business.

'I guess it makes this issue a bit less complicated,' she said. Especially given what the social
worker had suggested to her yesterday—something Emmy had baulked at, but which might
turn out to be a sensible solution now.

She took a sip of coffee. 'Maybe,' she said
slowly, 'Pete and Ally thought that between us
we could give Tyler what he needs.'

He narrowed his eyes at her. 'How do you
mean?'

'We have different strengths.' And different
weaknesses, but she wasn't going to point that
out. They were going to need to work together
on this, and now wasn't the time for a fight. 'We
can bring different things to his life.'

He folded his arms. 'So I do the serious stuff
and you do all the fun and glitter?'

Emmy had been prepared to compromise, but
this was too much. And this was exactly why
she'd disliked Dylan from practically the moment they'd met. Because he was judgemental,
arrogant, and had the social skills of a rhino.
Either he genuinely didn't realise what he'd just

said or he really didn't care—and she wasn't sure which. She lifted her chin. 'You mean, because I work with pretty, shiny things, they distract my poor little female brain from being able to focus on anything real?' she asked, her voice like cut glass.

His wince told her that he hadn't actually meant to insult her. 'Put that way, it sounds bad.'

'It *is* bad, Dylan. Look, you know I have my own business. If I was an airhead, unable to do a basic set of yearly accounts and work out my profit margins, then I'd be starving and in debt up to my eyeballs. Just to clarify the situation for you, that's not the case. My bank account's in the black and my business is doing just fine, thank you. Or will you be requiring a letter from my bank manager to prove that?'

He held her gaze. 'OK. I apologise. I shouldn't have said that.'

'Good. Apology accepted.' And maybe she should cut him some slack. He'd said that Pete was as close to him as a brother, so right now he was obviously hurting as much as she was. Especially as he was having to deal with a relationship break-up as well. And Dylan Harper was the most formal, uptight man Emmy had ever met, which meant he probably wasn't so good at emotional stuff. No doubt lashing out and making snippy remarks was his way of dealing with things. Letting it go—this time—didn't mean that she was going to let him walk all over her in the future.

'OK, so we don't get on; but this isn't actually about us. It's about a little boy who has nobody, and giving him a stable home where he can grow up knowing he's loved and valued.' And this wasn't the first time she and Dylan had had to put their differences aside. They'd managed it for Pete and Ally's wedding. When, come to think of it, Dylan's wife had been away on business and hadn't been able to attend, despite the fact that she worked with the groom and was married to the best man.

Emmy and Dylan had put their differences aside again two months ago, in the same ancient little church where Ally and Pete had got married, when they'd stood by the font and made their promises as godparents. Dylan's wife had been absent then, too. So maybe the marriage had been in trouble for a while, and Pete knew what was going on in Dylan's life. Which would make a bit more sense of the decision to ask both Dylan and Emmy to be Tyler's guardian.

She looked Dylan straight in the eye. 'I meant every word I said in church on my godson's christening day. I intend to be there for him.'

Was Emmy implying that he wasn't? Dylan felt himself bristling. 'I meant every word I said, too.'

'Right.'

But he couldn't discern an edge in her voice—at least, not like the one that had been there when he'd as good as called her an airhead. And that mollified him slightly. Maybe they could work together on this. Maybe she'd put the baby first instead of being the overemotional, needy mess she'd been when he'd first met her. Emmy wasn't serious and focused, like Nadine. She was un-structured and flaky. Something Dylan refused to put up with; he'd already had to deal with enough of that kind of behaviour in his life. No more.

'Look, Ally and Pete wanted us to take care of

their baby, if anything happened to them.' She swallowed hard. 'And the worst *has* happened.'

Dylan could see the sheen of tears in her grey eyes, and her lower lip actually started to wobble. Oh, no. Please don't let her cry. He wasn't good with tears. And he'd seen enough of them in those last few weeks with Nadine to last him a lifetime. If Emmy started crying, he'd have to walk out of the café. Because right now he couldn't cope with any more emotional pressure. As it was, he felt as if the world had slipped and he were slowly sliding backwards, unable to stop himself and with nothing to hang on to.

She dragged in a breath. 'We're going to have to work together on this and put our personal feelings aside.'

'Fair point.' They didn't have a lot of choice in the matter. And at least she was managing to hold the tears back. That was something. 'We'll work together.' Dylan was still slightly surprised at how businesslike she was being. This wasn't Emmy-like behaviour. She'd been late the first three times they'd met, and given the most feeble of excuses. And he'd lost count of the times he'd been over at Ally and Pete's and Ally had

had to rush off to pick up the pieces when yet another of Emmy's disastrous relationships had ended. It was way, way too close to the way his mother behaved, and Dylan had no patience for that kind of selfishness.

And his comment about the glitter hadn't been totally unfounded. He was pretty sure she'd choose to do the fun things with Tyler and leave him to do all the serious stuff. Emmy was all about fun. Which wasn't enough: sometimes you had to put the fun aside and do what needed to be done rather than what you wanted to do. 'So you've been looking after Tyler?'

'Since they left.' She shrugged. 'Babysitting.'

Except now it wasn't babysitting anymore. There wasn't anyone to hand Tyler back to.

She blew out a breath. 'The social worker came to see me last night. She said that Tyler needs familiarity and a routine. So I guess the first thing we need to do is to set up a routine, something as near as possible to what he's used to.'

Considering the chaos that usually surrounded Emmy Jacobs, Dylan couldn't imagine her setting up any kind of routine. But he bit his tongue. He'd already annoyed her today. Right now he needed to be conciliatory. For his god-son's sake. 'Right.'

'And, as the solicitor said, we're sharing custody.'

'Meaning that one week you have him, the next week I do?' Dylan suggested. 'Fine. That works for me.'

'It doesn't work at all.'

He frowned at her, not understanding. 'Why not?'

'Just as Tyler gets settled in with me, I have to bring him to you; and just as he gets settled with you, you have to bring him to me?' She shook her head. 'That's not fair on him.'

'So what are you suggesting?'

'The social worker,' she said, not meeting his gaze, 'suggested that Tyler stays in his own home. She says that whoever cares for him needs to, um, live there, too.'

He blinked. 'You're planning to move into Ally and Pete's house?'

She coughed. 'Not just me.'

What she was saying finally sank in. 'You're suggesting *we live together*?' The idea was so shocking, he almost dropped his coffee.

'No.' She lifted her chin, looking affronted. 'The social worker suggests that we share a house and share Tyler's care. Believe you me, it's not what I want to do—but it's the most sensible solution for Tyler. It saves us having to traipse a tired and hungry baby all over London at times that don't suit him. We'll be fitting round him, not the other way round.'

'Share a house. That sounds like living together, to me.' Something Dylan knew he wasn't good at. Hadn't he failed spectacularly with Nadine? His marriage had broken up because he hadn't wanted a family and the wife he'd loved had given him an ultimatum. A choice he couldn't accept. And now Emmy Jacobs— a woman who embodied everything he didn't like—seriously expected him to make a family with *her*?

'It isn't living together. It's just sharing a house.' Her mouth tightened, and she gave him a look as if to say that he was the last person on earth she'd choose to live with.

He needed to be upfront about this. 'I don't want to share a house with you,' he said.

'It's not my idea of fun, either, but what else—?'

She paused. 'Actually, no, there *is* an easy solution to this. You can agree to me having full-time care of Tyler.'

'That isn't what Pete and Ally wanted.' And he didn't think Emmy was stable enough to look after Tyler, not permanently. Then again, Dylan couldn't imagine himself taking care of Tyler, either. He knew practically nothing about babies. He'd never even babysat his godson. Pete and Ally had never asked him, knowing that his personal life was in chaos and his head wasn't in the right place. And Dylan was guiltily aware that he'd jumped at the excuse rather than face up to the fact that he wasn't a very good godfather.

He'd agreed to be Tyler's guardian. Of course he had. For the same reason that Emmy had agreed, probably, wanting to support his best friend. But he'd never thought it would actually happen. He'd considered himself to be a safety net that would never need to be used.

And now…

Lack of sleep. That was why his head was all over the place. There was a black hole where his best friend had once been. And now there were all these new demands on him and he wasn't sure he could meet them. He'd promised to be there for Tyler, and he hated himself for the fact that, now he actually had to make good on that promise, he didn't want to do it. He resented the way that a baby could wreak such havoc on his life and turn everything upside down; and then he felt guilty all over again for resenting someone so tiny and defenceless, because it wasn't the baby's fault and—well, he was being *selfish*.

Emmy was offering him a get-out. It would be, oh, so easy to take it. And yet Dylan knew that he'd never respect himself again if he took it—if he did what his mother had done, and dumped all his responsibilities on someone else. If he ignored a child who needed him.

'I know it isn't what Pete and Ally wanted,' Emmy said, clearly oblivious to the turmoil in Dylan's head. 'But it's not fair to keep uprooting Tyler, just to suit ourselves.'

'He's a baby. He's not even going to notice his surroundings,' Dylan said.

'Actually, he is. And if we did alternate weeks he'd have to get used to two different sets of rules, two different atmospheres. That's too much to expect.'

'And you're an expert on childcare?' he asked, knowing how nasty it sounded but unable to stop himself, because it was easier to fight with her than to admit how mixed up and miserable he felt right now.

'No. But I've read up on it. I've spent time with him. And I know how Ally wanted him brought up.'

'Fair point,' he muttered, feeling even more guilty. He hadn't done any of those things.

'You don't want to live with him, but you don't want to let me have full-time care of him, either.' She sighed. 'So what *do* you want, Dylan?'

'Pete and Ally back. Life as it was supposed to be.' The words came out before he could stop them.

'Well, unless you can turn into a superhero and spin the world round the other way to reverse time, and then stop the accident happening...' She looked away. 'Life isn't like the movies. I wish it could be. That I could wave a magic wand and everything would be OK again. But I can't. I'm a normal godmother, not a fairy godmother. And we have to do what's right for Tyler. To make his world as good as it can be, now his parents are gone and he has only us.'

She was right. Which made Dylan feel even more guilty. He was acting like a spoiled brat, crying for the moon and stars. And it was *wrong*. 'So what do you suggest?'

'The way I see it, we have two choices. Either we do what Pete and Ally wanted, and we find some way to be civil to each other while we bring up their child, or you let me bring him up on my own.'

'Or I could bring him up on my own,' Dylan suggested, nettled that she hadn't listed it as a third option.

She scoffed. 'So, what? You get a live-in nanny and dump his care on her, and see him for two seconds when you get home from work?'

'That's unfair.'

'Is it?' she asked pointedly.

He'd rather have all his teeth pulled out without anaesthetic than admit it to her, but it was probably accurate. 'I don't want to live with you.' He didn't want to live with anyone.

'Newsflash. I don't want to live with you, either. But I'm prepared to put Tyler's needs before mine. Just as I know Ally would've done for me, if our positions were reversed.'

And just as Pete would've done for him. Disgust at himself flared through Dylan's body. At heart, he really was a chip off the old block, as selfish as his mother. And that didn't sit well with him. He didn't want to be like her. 'Caring for a baby on your own is a hell of a commitment.'

'I know. But I'm prepared to do it.'

'Pete and Ally knew it was too much to ask one person to do. It's why they asked us both.'

'And you've had second thoughts.' She shrugged. 'Look, it's fine. I'll manage. I can always ask my mum for help.'

Which was a lot more than Dylan could do. And how pathetic was he to resent that?

'I need some time to think about this,' he said. Time where he could work things out, without anyone crowding his head. Where he could do what he always did when he made a business decision: work out all the scenarios, decide which one had the most benefits and least risks. Plan things without any emotions getting in the way and messing things up. 'How long is it until you need to get back to Tyler?'

'Mum said she could babysit for as long as I needed. I had no idea how long things would take at the solicitor's.'

He made a snap decision. 'OK. We'll meet again in an hour. When we've both had time to get our heads round it.'

'I don't need t—' she began, then shut up. 'You're right. I've had time to think about what the social worker said. You haven't. And it's a big deal. Of course you need time to think about it. Is an hour enough?'

He'd make sure it was. 'An hour's fine. I'll see you back here then.'

CHAPTER TWO

FRESH AIR. THAT would help, for starters. Dylan found the nearest park and walked, ignoring the noise from tourists and families.

Pros and cons. He didn't want to live with anyone. He was still licking his wounds from the end of his marriage—ironic, considering that he'd been the one to end it. And even more ironic that, if Nadine had waited six more months before issuing that ultimatum, she would've had her dream.

But it was too late, now. He couldn't go back. He didn't love her anymore, and he knew she was seeing someone else. Someone who was prepared to give her what he wouldn't. What hurt most now was that he'd failed at being a husband.

That left him with a slightly less complicated situation; though it didn't make his decision any easier. If he did have to live with someone else, an emotional, flaky woman and a tiny baby would be right at the bottom of his list. He had a business to run—something that took up as much of his energy as he could give. He didn't have *time* for a baby.

But...

If he backed out, if he let Emmy shoulder all the responsibilities and look after the baby, he'd only be able to block out the guilt for a short time. It would eat away at him, to the point where it would affect his business decisions and therefore the livelihoods of everyone who worked for him. Besides, how could he live with himself if he abandoned the child his best friend had loved so dearly?

Given how often he'd been dumped as a child, how could he do the same thing to this baby?

He couldn't let Tyler down. Couldn't break a promise he'd made.

Which meant he had to find a way of coexisting with Emmy.

She'd said earlier that they wouldn't be living together, just sharing a house. They could lead completely separate lives. All they'd need to do was to set up a rota for childcare and then brief each other at a handover. He could do that. OK, so he'd have to delegate more at work, to carve out that extra time, but it was doable. His flat was on a short-term lease, so that wasn't a problem. And he had no intention of getting involved with anyone romantically, so that wouldn't be a problem in the future, either.

So the decision was easy, after all.

He walked back to the café, and was slightly surprised to find that Emmy was already there. Or maybe she'd never left. Whatever.

'Coffee?' he asked. 'You paid last time, so this one's on me.'

'Thank you.'

He ordered coffee then joined her at the table. 'If we're going to share a house and Tyler's care, then we need to sort out some ground rules. Set up a rota.'

She rolled her eyes. 'Obviously. Childcare and housework.'

'Not housework. We'll get a housekeeper.'

She shook her head. 'I can't afford to pay a housekeeper.'

'I can. So that's settled.'

'No. This is shared equally. Time and bills.'

Did she have to be so stubborn about this? It was a practical decision. The idea was to look at how they could make this work, with the least pain to both of them. Why do something he didn't have time for and didn't enjoy, when he could pay someone to do it? 'Look, I'm going to have a hard enough time fitting a baby into my work schedule, without adding in extra stuff. And I'm sure it's the same for you. It makes sense to pay someone to clean the house and take some of the pressure off us.'

'I can probably stretch to paying someone to clean for a couple of hours a week,' she said, 'but that's as far as it goes.'

'So you're saying we both have to cook?'

'Well, obviously. It's a bit stupid, both of us cooking separately. It makes sense to share.' She stared at him. 'Are you telling me you can't cook?'

He shrugged. 'I shared a house with Pete at university.' And Emmy must know how hopeless Pete was—had been, Dylan corrected himself with a jolt—in the kitchen. 'So it was starve, eat nothing but junk, or learn to cook.'

'And what did you opt for?'

Did she *really* have to ask? He narrowed his eyes at her, just to make the point that she was being overpicky. 'I learned to cook. I only do basic stuff—don't expect Michelin-star standard—but it'll be edible and you won't get food poisoning.' He paused as a nasty thought struck him. 'Does that mean *you* don't cook?'

'I can do the basics,' she said. 'I shared a house with Ally at university.'

And Ally was an excellent cook. Dylan had never turned down the offer of a meal at his best friend's; he was pretty sure it must've been the same for Emmy. 'And she did all the cooking?' he asked.

'Our deal was that she cooked and I cleaned.' Emmy shrugged. 'Though I picked up a few tips from her along the way.'

But she wasn't claiming to be a superchef. Which made two of them. Basic food it would have to be. Which wasn't much change from the way he'd been living, the last six months. 'Right. So we'll pay a cleaner, and have a rota for childcare and cooking.'

He took a sip of his coffee, though it didn't do much to clear his head. Three days ago, he'd been just an ordinary workaholic. No commitments—well, *almost* no commitments, he amended mentally. No commitments once his divorce papers came through and he signed them.

Today, it was a different world. His best friend had died; and it looked as if he'd be sharing the care of his godson with a woman who'd always managed to rub him up the wrong way. Not the life he'd planned or wanted. But he was just going to have to make the best of it.

'So who looks after Tyler when we're at work?' he asked.

'We take turns.'

'I'm not with you.'

'Ally wasn't planning to go back to work until after his second birthday. She wanted to be a stay-at-home mum and look after her own baby.' Emmy looked awkward. 'I don't think she would've wanted us to put him in day care or get a nanny.'

'We're not Ally and Pete, so we're going to have to make a decision that works for both of us,' Dylan pointed out. 'We both have a business to run. Taking time off work isn't going to happen. Not if we want to keep our businesses running.'

'Unless,' Emmy suggested, 'we work flexible hours. Delegate, if we have to.'

'Delegate?' He frowned. 'I thought you were a sole trader?'

'I am, but you're not.'

He almost asked her if she was using the royal 'we', and stopped himself just in time. That wasn't fair. She was trying. And he bit back the snippy comment that she was trying in more than one sense of the word.

'Are you a morning or an evening person?' she asked.

He usually worked both. That had been another of Nadine's complaints: Dylan was a work-aholic who was always in the office or in his study. 'Either.'

'I prefer working in the evenings. So, if you're not bothered, how about you go in early and I'll take care of Tyler; and then you take over from me at, say, half-three, so I can get on with my work?'

'And what if I need to have a late meeting?'

'We can be flexible,' she said. 'But if you're

late back one day, then you'll have to be home much earlier, the next day, to give me that time back.' She shrugged. 'There might be times when I have meetings and need you to take over from me. So I guess we're going to have to be flexible, work as a team, and cover for each other when we need to.'

Work as a team with a woman he'd always disliked. A woman who reminded him of the worst aspects of his mother—the sort who'd dump her responsibilities on someone else with no notice so she could drift off somewhere to 'find herself'.

Dylan pinched himself, just to check that this wasn't some peculiar nightmare. But it hurt. So there was no waking up from this situation.

'OK. We'll sort out a rota between us.' He paused. 'I still don't want to live with you, but I guess the only option is to share the house.' It didn't mean they had to share any time together outside the handover slots.

'So when do we move in to Pete and Ally's?' she asked

'I have to sort out the lease on my flat,' he said. 'And I'll need to talk to the bank about subletting my flat, to make sure it doesn't affect the mortgage.'

Dylan was surprised. He hadn't thought Emmy would be together enough to buy her own place.

'And they might be able to put me in touch with a good letting agency,' she finished.

She'd obviously thought this through. Then again, she'd had time to think about it. The social worker had talked to her about it already.

'So we could move in tomorrow.'

He'd rather not move in at all, but he had no choice. Not if he was going to carry out his duty. 'Tomorrow.' He paused. 'Look—we really need to put Tyler first. We don't like each other, but we've agreed to make an effort for his sake. What happens if we really can't get on?'

'I don't know.'

'In a business, if you hire someone in a senior role, you'd have a trial period to make sure you suited each other. Then you'd review it and decide on the best way forward.'

'This isn't a job, Dylan.'

'I know, but I think a trial period might be the fairest way for all of us. Give it three months. See if we can make it work.'

She nodded. 'And, if we can't, then you'll agree that I'll have sole care of Tyler?'

He wasn't ready to agree to that. 'We'll review it,' he said. 'See what the viable options are.'

'OK. Three months.' She paused. 'But if anything big comes up, we discuss it before the situation gets out of hand.'

That worked for him. 'Agreed.'

'So that's settled.' She lifted her chin. 'Before we go any further, I need to know something. Is there anyone who'd be upset about us sharing a house?'

He frowned. 'I've already told you, I'm separated from Nadine. It won't be a problem.'

'What about the woman you had an affair with?'

He stared at her in disbelief. 'What woman?'

'Oh, come on. It's the main reason why marriages break down. Someone has an affair. Usually the man.'

Was she really that cynical?

Had that happened to her?

He couldn't remember Pete or Ally ever talking about going to Emmy's wedding, but at the end of the day a marriage certificate was just a piece of paper. Maybe Emmy had been living with someone who'd let her down in that way. 'Not that it's any of your business why my marriage broke up, but for the record neither of us had an affair,' he said tightly.

Colour stained her cheeks, 'I apologise.'

Which was something, he supposed. 'There's nobody who would be affected by us sharing a house,' he said quietly.

Or was there another reason why she'd asked? A way to introduce the subject, maybe, because there was someone in her life who'd be upset? 'If it's a problem for you, I'm happy to—'

'There's nobody,' she cut in.

Was it his imagination, or did she suddenly look tired and miserable and lonely?

No. He was just reflecting how he felt on her. Tired and miserable, because he'd barely slept since the news of the crash; and lonely, because the one person Dylan could've talked to about this—well, he'd been *in* that crash and he wasn't here anymore.

'Though I could do without a string of dates being paraded through the house,' she added.

He raised an eyebrow. 'I'm not quite divorced

yet. Do you really think I'm dating?' Despite the fact that he knew his almost-ex wife was, he wasn't.

She grimaced. 'Sorry. I take that back. It's not your fault I have a rubbish taste in men. I shouldn't tar you with the same brush as them.'

He'd been right, then. Someone had let her down. More than one, he'd guess.

Dylan had never noticed before, probably because he'd been more preoccupied with being annoyed by her, but Emmy Jacobs was actually pretty. Slender, with a fine bone structure highlighted by her gamine haircut. Her hair was defiantly plum: not a natural shade, but it suited her, bringing out the depths in her huge grey eyes.

Though what on earth was he doing, thinking about Emmy in those sorts of terms?

Better put it down to the shock of bereavement. He and Emmy might be about to share a house and the care of a baby, but that was as far as it would go. They'd be lucky to keep things civil between them. And he definitely wasn't in the market for any kind of relationship. Been there, done that, and failed spectacularly. It had taught him to steer clear, in future. He was better off

on his own. It meant there was nobody to disap-
point. Nobody to walk away, the way his mother
had and Nadine had.

'I assume you have a set of keys to Pete and
Ally's house?' he asked.

She nodded. 'You, too?'

'So I could keep an eye on the place while
they're not there. For emergencies. Which I always thought would be a burst pipe or something like that. Not…' His throat closed, and he
couldn't get the words out. For the first time in
years, he was totally speechless.

To his surprise, Emmy reached across the table
to take his hand and squeezed it briefly. With
sympathy, not pity. 'Me, too. I keep thinking
I'm going to wake up and discover that this is
all just some incredibly realistic nightmare and
everything's just fine. Except I've woken up too
many times already and found out that it's not.'

Whatever her faults—and Dylan knew there
were a lot of them—Emmy's feelings for Ally
and Pete were in no doubt. Surprising himself
further, he returned the squeeze. 'And we've still
got the funeral to go through.'

She sighed and withdrew her hand. 'I guess their parents will want to arrange it.'

'You said yourself, Pete's dad is elderly and Ally's mum isn't well. They'll need support. I was going to offer to sort it out for them. If they tell me what they want, I can arrange it.'

'That's good of you to take the burden off their shoulders.' She took a deep breath. 'Count me in on the support front. Anything you need me to do, tell me and I'll do it.'

She wasn't being polite, Dylan knew. The tears were shimmering in her eyes again. And he wanted to get out of here as fast as he could, before she actually started crying. 'Thanks. I guess we'd better exchange phone numbers. Home, work, whatever.'

She nodded, and took her mobile phone from her handbag. It was a matter of seconds to give each other the details. 'And we'll meet at the house after work tomorrow to sort out the rota.'

'OK. I'll call you when I'm on my way.'

'Thanks.' She drained her cup. 'I'd better get back to Tyler. See you later.'

He watched her walk out of the café. The woman who annoyed him more than anyone he'd ever met. The woman he was going to move in with tomorrow.

Yeah, life was really throwing him a curve-ball. And he was just going to have to deal with it. Somehow.

The next morning, Emmy unlocked the door to Pete and Ally's three-storey Georgian house in Islington, pressed in the code for the alarm, and put her small suitcase down in the hallway.

'It's just you and me for now, Ty,' she said softly to the baby, who was securely strapped into his sling and cradled against her heart. 'We're home. Except—' her breath caught '—it's going to be with me and Dylan looking after you, from now on, instead of your mum and dad.'

It still felt wrong. But over the course of the day she managed to make a list of the rest of the things she needed to bring from her flat, feed Tyler, give him a bath and put him to bed in his cot, and make a basic spaghetti sauce for dinner so that all she'd have to do was heat it through and cook some pasta when Dylan turned up after he'd finished work.

Home.

Would she ever come to think of this place as home? Emmy thought with longing of her own flat in Camden. It was small, but full of light; and it was *hers*. From next week, a stranger would be living there and enjoying the views over the local park. And she would be living here in a much more spacious house—the sort she would never have been able to afford on her own—with Dylan and Tyler.

Almost like a family.

Just what she'd always wanted.

Well, she didn't want *Dylan*, she amended. But Emmy had envied part of her best friend's life: having a husband who loved her and a gorgeous baby. Something Emmy had wanted, herself. A real family.

'But I didn't want to have it *this* way, Ally,' she said softly. 'I wanted someone of my own. Someone who wouldn't let me down.' Someone that maybe somebody else should've picked for her, given how bad her own choices of life partner had been in the past.

And that family she was fantasising about was just that: a fantasy. The baby wasn't really hers, and neither was the house. And she was sharing the house with Dylan Harper, as a co-guardian. She couldn't think of anyone less likely to be the love of her life, just as she knew that she was the exact opposite of the kind of women Dylan liked. Chalk and cheese wasn't the half of it.

But then again, Tyler might not be her flesh and blood, but he was her responsibility now. Her godson. A baby she'd known for every single day of his little life. A baby she'd cradled in her arms when he was only a few hours old, sitting on the side of her best friend's hospital bed and feeling the same surge of love she'd felt for the woman who'd been as close as a sister to her.

She drew her knees up to her chin and wrapped her arms round her legs, blinking away the tears. 'I promise you I'll love Tyler as if he was my own, Ally,' she said softly into the empty room. 'I'll do my best by him.'

She just hoped that her best would be good enough. Though this was one thing she really couldn't afford to fail at. There wasn't a plan B.

The lights on the baby listener glowed steadily, and Emmy couldn't hear a thing; Tyler was obviously sound asleep. She glanced at her watch.

Hopefully Dylan wouldn't be too much longer. In the meantime, she had a job to do. She uncurled and headed back to the kitchen, where she took a large piece of card and marked it out into a two-week rota for childcare and chores. She worked steadily, putting in different coloured sticky notes to show which were her slots and which were Dylan's.

All the way through, she kept glancing at her watch. There was still no sign of Dylan, and it was getting on to half-past seven.

This was ridiculous. Had he forgotten that he was meant to be here, sorting things out with her? Or was he just in denial?

And to think he'd pegged himself as the sensible, organised one.

Yeah, right.

Irritated, she picked up her mobile phone and rang him.

He answered within two rings. 'Dylan Harper.' Though he sounded absent, as if his attention was elsewhere.

'It's Emmy,' she said crisply. 'Emmy Jacobs.' Just in case he was trying to block that out, too.

There was a pause. 'Oh.'

'Are you not supposed to be somewhere right now?' She made her voice supersaccharine.

'You suggested we meefairt at the house today after work.'

'Mmm-hmm. Which is where I am now. So are you expecting me to stay up until midnight or whenever you can be bothered to turn up and sort things through?'

He sighed. 'Don't nag.'

Nag? If he'd been fair about this, she wouldn't have to nag. 'This is meant to be about team-work, Dylan. There's no "I" in team,' she reminded him.

'Oh, spare me the clichés, Emmy,' he drawled.

Her patience finally gave out. 'Just get your backside over here so we can sort things out,' she said, and hung up.

CHAPTER THREE

IT WAS ANOTHER hour before Emmy heard the front door open, and by that point she was ready to climb the walls with frustration.

Be conciliatory, she reminded herself. Do this for Pete and Ally. And Tyler. Even though you want to smack the man over the head with a wok, you have to be nice. At least for now. Make things work. It's only for three months, and then he'll realise that it'd be best if you looked after Tyler on your own. Come on, Emmy. You can do this. *Smile.*

'Good evening. Is pasta OK with you for dinner?' she asked when he walked into the kitchen.

He looked surprised. 'You cooked dinner for me?'

'As I was here, yes. By the way, that means it's your turn to cook for us tomorrow.'

'Uh-huh.' He looked wary.

'One thing you need to know. If I get hungry,

I get grumpy.' She gave him a level stare. 'Don't make me wait in future. You *really* won't like me then.' Which was a bit ironic. He didn't like her now, and he hadn't even seen her on a really bad day.

'You could've eaten without me,' he said. 'I wouldn't have minded just reheating something in the microwave.'

'I had no idea how long you were going to be, and I would've felt bad if you'd turned up while I was halfway through eating my dinner.' She paused. 'Do you really work an hour's commute away from here?'

'No. I work in Docklands. About half an hour away.' At least he had the grace to look embarrassed. 'I had to finish something, first.'

She blew out a breath. 'OK. Take the lecture as read. We're sharing Tyler's care so, in future, you're either going to have to learn to delegate, or you'll have to work from home when the baby's napping.'

Hearing his godson's name seemed to galvanise Dylan. 'Where is he?'

'Asleep in his cot.' She gestured to the kitchen table. 'Sit down. I've made a start on the rota, given what we discussed yesterday morning. Perhaps you can review it while I finish cooking dinner, and move any of the sticky notes if you need to.'

'Sticky notes?' He looked puzzled.

'Because it's a provisional rota. Sticky notes mean it's easy to move things around without the rota getting messy. Once we've agreed our slots, I'll write it in properly. I'll get it laminated. And then we can use sticky notes day by day to make any changes to the rota—that way it'll be an obvious change so we'll both remember it.'

'OK.' He looked at her. 'Sorry.'

Dylan Harper had apologised to her? That was a first. Actually, no, it was the second time he'd said sorry to her in as many days. And, even though Emmy thought that he more than owed her that apology just now, she decided to be gracious about it. Be the bigger person. 'It's a bit of a radical lifestyle change for both of us. I think it'll take us a while to get used to it.'

He nodded. 'True.'

She concentrated on cooking the pasta and heating the sauce, then served up their meal at the kitchen table.

He put the card to one side. 'The rota looks fine to me. I notice it's a two-week one.'

'I thought that would be fair, giving each other alternate weekends off.'

'Yes, that's fair,' he agreed. He ate a mouthful of the pasta. 'And this is good. Thank you. I wasn't expecting dinner. I was going to make myself a sandwich or something.'

She knew exactly where he was coming from. 'I do that too often. It doesn't feel worth cooking for one, does it?'

'Especially if cooking isn't your thing.' He blew out a breath. 'I never expected to be living with—well, *you*.'

He'd made that perfectly clear. He really didn't have to harp on about it. 'We'll just have to make the best of it, for Tyler's sake,' she said dryly.

'Agreed. How did you get on with the mortgage and the letting agency?' he asked.

'It's all sorted. I'm letting my flat in Camden from Monday. You?'

'It's a short-term lease. Nadine has the house.'

His wife. 'Have you told her about this?'

His expression said very clearly, *that's none of your business*, and she shut up. No, it wasn't her business. And he'd already said that nobody would be upset by him sharing a house and Tyler's care with her.

'I'll go back to my place tonight to pick up the basics, and move the rest in over the next few days.' He looked at her. 'I assume you've done the same?'

'Yes to the basics today, but I haven't chosen a room yet. I was waiting for you.' She grimaced. 'I'm really glad Ally and Pete have two spare bedrooms as well as the nursery. I don't think I could face using their room.'

'Me, neither.' He shrugged. 'Which of the spare rooms I have doesn't bother me. Pick whichever one you like.'

'Thanks.' Though it wasn't the bedroom that concerned her most. 'Can I use Pete's study? I work from home,' she explained, 'and I need somewhere to set up my equipment. And that means a room with decent lighting.'

She was glad she'd been conciliatory when he said, 'That's fine by me. I can work anywhere with a laptop and a briefcase. So you have, what, some kind of workbench?'

It was the first time he'd ever shown any interest in her work, and it unnerved her slightly. She wasn't used to Dylan being anything other than abrupt to her. 'Yes, and I have a desk where I sketch the pieces before I make them. And before Tyler gets mobile I'll need to get a baby gate fixed on the doorway. I don't want him anywhere near my tools because they're sharp and dangerous.' She looked at him. 'Are you any good at DIY?'

'No. I'd rather pay someone to do it,' he said.

That was refreshing. The men she'd dated in the past had all taken the attitude that having a Y chromosome meant that they'd automatically be good at DIY, and they weren't prepared to admit when they were hopeless and couldn't even put a shelf on straight. Then again, she wasn't actually dating Dylan. He might be easy on the eye—she had to admit that he was good-looking—but he was the last man she'd ever want to date. He was way too uptight. 'OK. I know the number of a good handyman. I'll get it sorted.'

He looked at their empty plates. 'I haven't organised a cleaner yet.'

'And I wouldn't expect a cleaner to do dirty

dishes,' Emmy said crisply. 'Especially as Ally and Pete have a dishwasher.'

'Point taken. I'll stack the dishwasher, then go and pick up my stuff.'

She chose her room while he was out, opting for the room she'd stayed in several times as a guest. It was strange to think that—unless things changed dramatically during their three-month trial—she'd be living here until Tyler had grown up. And even stranger to think she'd be sharing the house with Dylan Harper. Even if it might only be for a short time.

Still, she'd made a promise to Ally. She wouldn't back out.

She unpacked the small case she'd brought with her, then checked on Tyler. He was still sound asleep. Unable to resist, she reached down to touch his cheek. Such soft, soft skin. And he was so vulnerable. She and Dylan really couldn't let him down, whatever their doubts about each other. 'Sleep tight, baby,' she whispered, and went downstairs to the kitchen to wait for Dylan. She'd left the baby listener on; she glanced at it to make sure the lights were working, then put a cello concerto on low and began to sketch some

ideas for the commission she'd been working on
before the whole world had turned upside down.

When Dylan came back to the house, he was
surprised to discover that Emmy was still up.
He hadn't expected her to wait up for him. Or
was she checking up on him or trying to score
some weird kind of point?

'Is Tyler OK?' he asked.

She nodded. 'He's fast asleep.'

'Whose turn is it on the rota for night duty?'
Then he grimaced. 'Forget I asked that. You've
been looking after him since Ally and Pete went
to Venice, so I'll go tonight if he wakes. Do I
need to sleep on the floor in his room?'

'No. There's a portable baby listener.' She indicated the device with lights that was plugged in
next to the kettle. 'Plug it in near your bed, and
you'll hear him if he wakes. The lights change
when there's a noise—the louder the noise, the
more lights come on. So that might wake you,
too.'

'Is he, um, likely to wake?' He didn't have a
clue about how long babies slept or what their
routines were. Pete had never talked about it,

and Dylan hadn't really had much to do with babies in the past. His mother was an only child, so there had been no babies in his family while he'd been growing up; and Pete was the first of his friends to have a child. Babies just hadn't featured in his life.

Although he'd accused Emmy of leaving him to do the serious stuff, he was guiltily aware that he'd never babysat his godson or anything like that, and she clearly had. She'd been a better godparent than he had, by far—much more hands-on. He'd just been selfish and avoided it.

'He'd just started to sleep through, a couple of weeks back; but I guess he's picked up on the tension over the last few days because he's woken every night since the accident.' Emmy sighed. 'He might need a nappy change or some milk, or he might just want a cuddle.'

'How do you know what he needs?' Babies were too little to tell you. They just screamed.

'The nappy, you'll definitely know,' she said dryly. 'Just sniff him.'

'*Sniff* him?' Had she really said that?

She smiled. 'Trust me, you'll know if he has a dirty nappy. If he's hungry, he'll keep bumping his face against you and nuzzling for milk. And if he just wants a cuddle, hold him close and he'll settle and go to sleep. Eventually.'

'Poor little mite.' Dylan felt a muscle clench in his cheek. 'I hate that Pete's never going to get to know his son. He's not going to see him grow up. He's not going to teach him to ride a bike or swim. He's not going to…' He blew out a breath. 'I just hate all this.'

'Me, too,' she said softly. 'I hate that Ally's going to miss all the firsts. The first tooth, the first word, the first steps. All the things she was so looking forward to. She was keeping a baby book with every single detail.'

'I never thought I'd ever be a dad. It wasn't in my life plan.' Dylan grimaced. 'And I haven't exactly been a hands-on godparent, so far. Not the way you've been. I'm ashamed to say it, but I don't have a clue where I should even start right now.'

'Most men aren't that interested in babies until they have their own,' she said. 'Don't beat yourself up about it too much.'

'I've never even changed a nappy before,' he

KATE HARDY   59

confessed. There really hadn't been the need or
the opportunity.

'Are you trying to get out of doing night duty?'

Was she teasing him or was she going to throw
a hissy fit? He really wasn't sure. He couldn't
read her at all. Emmy was almost a stranger, and
now she was going to be a huge part of his life,
at least for the next three months. Unwanted, un-
looked for. A woman who'd always managed to
rub him up the wrong way. And he was going
to have to be nice to her, to keep the peace for
Tyler's sake. 'No,' he said, 'I'm not trying to
get out of it. But you know what you're doing—
you've looked after Tyler for the last few days
on your own. And I was just thinking, it might
be an idea if you teach me what I need to do.'

She blinked at him. 'You want *me* to teach
you?' She tested the words as if she didn't believe he'd just said them.

'If I don't have a business skill I need, I take a
course to learn it. This is the same sort of thing.
It might save us both a lot of hassle,' he said
dryly. 'And I think it'd be better if you show me
in daylight rather than tell me now. You know
the old stuff about teaching someone—I hear

and I forget, I see and remember, I do and I understand.'

She nodded. 'Fair enough. I'll keep the baby listener with me tonight. But, tomorrow, please make sure you're back early so I can teach you the basics—how to change a nappy, make up a bottle of formula, and do a bath. By early, I mean before five o'clock.'

When was the last time he'd left the office before seven? He couldn't remember. Tough. Tomorrow, he'd just have to make the effort. 'Deal,' he said.

'OK. See you tomorrow.'

He realised that she'd been working when she closed a folder and picked up a handful of pencils. But then again, hadn't she said something about preferring to work in the evening? So he squashed the growing feeling of guilt. She was self-employed. A sole trader who didn't need to keep to traditional business hours. She obviously worked the hours that suited her.

'See you tomorrow,' he said. 'Which room did you pick?'

'The one opposite Tyler's.'

Which left the one next to Pete and Ally's

room for him. 'OK. Thanks.' And then he realised he hadn't brought any bedding with him.

'The bed's already made up,' she said. 'I used
linen from Ally and Pete's airing cupboard. I
don't think they'd mind and it'd be a waste not
to use it.'

He pushed a hand through his hair. 'Sorry. I
didn't realise I'd said that aloud.'

'It's a lot to take in. A lot of change.' She
shrugged. 'We'll muddle through.'

'Yeah. Sleep well.' Which was a stupid thing
to say; of course she wouldn't, because Tyler
would wake up.

But she didn't look annoyed. Her eyes actually crinkled at the corners. Again, Dylan was
struck by the fact that Emmy Jacobs was pretty.
And again it tipped him off balance. He couldn't
even begin to think about Emmy in that way; it
would make things far too complicated.

'Sleep well, Dylan,' she said, and strolled out
of the kitchen.

Given how late Dylan had been the previous
night, and the fact that Emmy had asked him to
be back before five, he thought he'd better take

the afternoon off to deal with the baby-care is-
sues. He walked in to the house to find Emmy
playing with the baby and singing to him, while
the baby gurgled and smiled at her.

This felt distinctly weird. He'd never been
that interested in babies and he'd never wanted
a family of his own—which was most of the
reason why he'd married Nadine, because she'd
been just as dedicated to her career as he was
and didn't pose any kind of emotional risk. Or so
he'd thought. He hadn't expected her to change
her mind and give him an ultimatum: give me
a baby or give me a divorce. He didn't want a
baby, so the choice was obvious.

And now he was here. Instead of being in his
minimalist Docklands bachelor flat, he was living in a family home. Sharing the care of a tiny,
defenceless baby. And he didn't have the least
idea about what he was doing.

Emmy looked up at him. 'Hey, Ty, look, it's
Uncle Dylan.' She smiled. 'You're back early.'

It was the first time Dylan could ever remember Emmy smiling spontaneously at him, as if
she were genuinely pleased to see him, and he
was shocked that it made him feel warm inside.

Was he going crazy, reacting like this to her?

No, of course not. It was just because he'd been knocked off balance by Pete and Ally's death. Grief made him want to hold someone, that was all; to feel connected to the world, still. He was *not* becoming attracted to Emmy Jacobs. Even though he was beginning to think that maybe she wasn't quite who he'd always thought she was.

'We agreed you were going to teach me about nappies and baths,' he said. 'And you asked me to come back early. Here I am.' He spread his hands. 'So let's get it sorted.'

She blew a raspberry on Tyler's tummy, making the baby giggle. 'He's clean at the moment, so we might as well hold off on that side until he really needs a nappy change. But he's wide awake, so you can play with him.'

'Play with him?' Dylan repeated. He knew it was ridiculous—he was the head of a very successful computer consultancy and could sort out tricky business problems quickly and effectively. But he didn't have a clue about how to play with a baby. He'd never done it. Never needed to do it.

She rolled her eyes. 'Dylan, you can't just sit

and work on your laptop when you're in charge and Ty's awake. You need to play with him. Read to him. Talk to him.'

Dylan frowned. 'Isn't he a bit young for books?'

'No. Pete used to read to him,' she said softly. 'Ally read up about it and she wanted Tyler to have a good male role model. So Pete always did the bedtime story.'

OK. Reading to a baby couldn't be that hard. Talking, too. But playing...where did you start? He didn't know any baby games. Any nursery rhymes.

As if the panic showed on his face, she smiled at him. 'Come and give him a cuddle.'

And this was where Dylan got nervous. Where things could go terribly wrong. Because he didn't have a clue what he was doing. And he hated the fact that he had to take advice from someone as flaky as Emmy, because she clearly knew more about babies than he did. 'Do I have to hold his head or something?'

'No. He's four months old, not a newborn, so he can support his head just fine. He can't sit up on his own yet, but that'll happen in a few weeks.' She looked at him. 'OK. You might want to change.'

'Why?'

'Unless you don't mind your suit getting creased and needing to go to the cleaner's more often.'

The question must've been written all over his face, because she added, 'You're going to be on the floor with him a lot.'

She had a point. 'I'll be down in a minute.' Dylan took the stairs two at a time to his room, then changed into jeans and T-shirt.

When he came downstairs, she gave him an approving look. 'Righty. He's all yours.'

Panic seeped through Dylan. What was he meant to do now?

She kissed the baby. 'See you later, sweetie. Have fun with Uncle Dylan.' And then she went to hand the baby to him.

He could muddle through this.

But it was important to get it *right*.

'Uh—Emmy.' He really hated this, but what choice did he have? It was ask, or mess it up. 'I don't know what to do.'

She rolled her eyes. 'We've already discussed this. Play with him. It's not rocket science.'

She wasn't going to make this easy for him, was she? 'I haven't had anything to do with babies before.'

She scoffed. 'He's four months old and he's your godson. Of course you've spent time with him.'

'He's always been asleep or Ally was feeding him. Pete and I didn't do baby stuff together, not like you and Ally.'

She looked at him and nodded. 'It must really stick in your craw to have to ask *me* for help. And if I was a different kind of woman, I'd just walk away and let you get on with it. But Tyler's needs come first, so I'll help you.'

'For his sake, not mine. I get it. But thank you anyway.'

'So how come you're so clueless? Pete always said you were the brightest person he knew— Ally, too. And you're the same age as the rest of us. I don't understand how, at thirty-five years old, you can know absolutely nothing about babies.'

Although he knew there was a compliment in

there, of sorts, at the same time her words were damning. And he was surprised to find himself explaining. 'I'm an only child. No cousins, no close family.' At least, not since his grandmother died. His mother had never been close to him. 'Pete and Ally were the first of my friends to have children, and I...' He sighed. 'I guess I've been a bit preoccupied, the last few months.'

'Relationship break-ups tend to do that to you.' She looked rueful. 'And yes, I know that from way too much experience. OK. I never thought I'd need to show you any of this, but these are the kinds of things he likes to do with me.' She sat on the floor and balanced Tyler on her knees. 'Humpty Dumpty sat on the wall. Humpty Dumpty had a great...' She paused, and the baby clearly knew what was coming because he was beaming his head off. 'Fall,' she said, lowering her knees as she straightened her legs, and managing to keep the baby upright at the same time.

Her reward was a rich chuckle from the baby.

Something else that made him feel odd. 'And you always do the pause?' he asked, to take his focus off his feelings. This was about learning to care for a baby, not how he felt.

'I do. He's learned to anticipate it. He loved doing this with Ally. She used to string it out for ages.' She blew a raspberry on the baby's tummy, making him laugh, and handed him to Dylan. 'Your turn.'

'Humpty Dumpty sat on the wall,' Dylan intoned, feeling absolutely ridiculous and wishing he were a hundred miles away. Or, better still, back at his desk—where at least he knew what he was doing. 'Humpty Dumpty had a great...' He glanced at Emmy, who nodded. 'Fall,' he finished, and straightened his legs, letting the baby whoosh downwards but supporting him so he didn't fall.

Tyler laughed.

And something around Dylan's heart felt as if it had cracked.

There was a look of sheer wonder on Dylan's face as Tyler laughed up at him. He really hadn't been exaggerating about being a hands-off godfather, and this was obviously the first time he'd actually sat down with the baby and played with him. Emmy had the feeling that Dylan Harper, the stuffiest man in the world, kept everyone at arm's length. Well, you couldn't do that when you lived with a baby. So this was really going to change Dylan. It might make him human, instead of being a judgemental, formal machine.

When he did the Humpty Dumpty game for the third time, and laughed at the same time as the baby, she knew he was *definitely* changing. Tyler was about to turn Dylan Harper's life upside down again—but this time, in a good way.

'OK for me to go to work?' she asked.

'Sure. And, um, thanks for the lesson.' He still looked awkward and embarrassed, but at least they'd managed to be civil to each other.

Hopefully they could keep it up.

'No problem,' she said. 'I'll be in Pete's study if you get stuck with anything.'

CHAPTER FOUR

DYLAN WAS SURPRISED to discover how much he enjoyed playing with the baby. How good it was to hear that rich chuckle and know that he'd given Tyler a moment of pure happiness. If anyone had told him three weeks ago that he'd be having fun waving a toy duck around and quacking loudly, he would've dismissed it as utter insanity. But, this afternoon, it was a revelation.

He was actually disappointed when Tyler fell asleep.

Though it wasn't for long. The baby woke again and started crying, and Dylan picked him up almost on instinct. Then he wrinkled his nose. Revolting. It looked as if he needed another lesson from Emmy. He went to find her in Pete's study.

'Problem?' she asked.

'He needs a nappy change. Can you show me how to do it?'

'Ah, no. You're the one who said, "I do and I understand" is the best. I'll talk you through it.'

When they went upstairs to the nursery, Emmy did at least help Dylan get the baby out of his little all-in-one suit, for which he was grateful. But then she stood back and talked him through the actual process of nappy-changing.

How could someone so small produce something so—so *stinky*? he wondered.

He used wipe after wipe to clean the baby.

And it was only when he realised Emmy was grinning that he thought there might've been another way of doing it—one that maybe didn't use half a box of wipes at a time. 'So you're perfect at this, are you?' he asked, slightly put out.

'No—it usually takes me three or four wipes. Though Ally used to be able to do it in one.' Her smile faded, and she helped him put Tyler back in his Babygro.

'I'm going to do some work,' she said. 'Call me when Tyler needs a bath. His routine's on the board in the kitchen, so you'll know when he's due for a feed. If he's grizzly before then, try him with a drink. There's some cooled boiled water in sterilised bottles in the fridge.'

Again, Dylan was surprised by Emmy's effi-
ciency. Maybe he'd misjudged her really badly,
or he'd just seen her on bad days in the past—a
lot of bad days—and taken her the wrong way.

'Oh, and you need to wind him after a feed,'
she added. 'Hold him upright against your shoulder, rub his back, and he'll burp for you.'

'Got it.'

'Are you sure you can do this?'

No. He wasn't sure at all. But he didn't want
Emmy to think that he was bailing out already.
'Sure,' he lied.

He carried Tyler downstairs and checked the
routine board in the kitchen—which Emmy had
somehow managed to get written up properly
and laminated while he'd been at work. Apparently the baby needed a nap for about an hour;
then he'd need a bath and then finally a feed.

And it was also his turn to make dinner.

He hadn't even thought about buying food.
He'd only focused on the fact that he'd needed
to get everything done and leave the office ridiculously early. He opened the fridge door, and
was relieved to discover that there were ingre-
dients for a stir-fry. And there were noodles and

soy sauce in the cupboard. OK. He could work with that.

Now, how did you get a baby to sleep?

He sat down, settling Tyler against his arm. Sure, he'd given his godson a brief cuddle before, but Ally had understood that he wasn't used to babies and wasn't much good at this, so she hadn't given him a hard time about it. But it also meant she hadn't talked to him about baby stuff. And Emmy had just left him to it.

'I have no idea what to do now,' he said to the baby.

Tyler just gave him a gummy smile.

'Emmy seems to know what to do with you. But I don't.' OK, so he'd enjoyed playing with the baby, but was that all you were supposed to do?

'She's abandoned us,' he said, and then grimaced. 'And that's not very fair of me. If she'd stayed, I would've assumed she didn't trust me to do a good enough job with you and was being a control freak. So she can't win, whatever she does.'

Maybe he needed a new approach to Emmy. And she had given up some of her work time to show him how to care for Tyler. As she'd pointed out, she could've left him to muddle through and fall flat on his face, then gloated when he'd made a mess of things. But she hadn't. She'd played nice.

Maybe she was nice. Maybe he hadn't really given her a chance, before.

'I don't know any nursery rhymes,' he told the baby. Except for "Humpty Dumpty". He made a mental note to buy a book and learn some. 'I could tell you about computer programming.'

Another gummy smile.

'Binary code. Fibonacci sequence. Debugging.' He could talk for hours about that. 'Algorhythms.'

Well, the baby wasn't crying. That was a good thing, right? Dylan carried on talking softly to Tyler, until eventually the baby's eyes closed.

Now what? Did he just sit here until the baby woke up again? Or did he put the baby to sleep in his cot? He wished he'd thought to ask Emmy earlier. It wouldn't be fair to disturb her now. She needed time to get on with her work. And he could really do with checking his emails. OK. He'd put the baby down.

Gingerly, he managed to move out of the chair and placed the baby on his playmat. The mat was nice and soft, and Tyler would be safe there. Did he need a blanket? But his little hands felt warm. Maybe not, then.

While Tyler slept, Dylan caught up with some work on his laptop.

Not that it was easy to concentrate. He kept glancing over at the baby to check that everything was all right.

Eventually Tyler woke, and Dylan saved the file before closing the laptop and picking the baby up. 'Bath time. We need to go and find Emmy.'

He carried the baby through to Pete's study. The door was open, and soft classical music was playing. Another surprise; he'd pegged Emmy as someone who would listen to very girly pop music, the kind of stuff that was in the charts and that he loathed. Although he'd gone into the office earlier, he hadn't really taken any notice. He'd never seen her in a professional environment before, and there was a different air about her. Total focus and concentration as she worked on something that looked very intricate.

If he interrupted her now, would it make her jump and wreck what she was doing?

He waited, jiggling the baby as he'd seen her do, until her hands moved away, and then he knocked on the open door. 'You said to come and get you when Tyler woke up and it was bath time.'

She looked up from her workbench, smiled, and put her tools down. 'Sure.'

He caught a glimpse of the work on her bench; it looked like delicate silver filigree. Again, it wasn't what he'd expected from her; he'd thought that she'd make in-your-face ethnic-style jewellery, or lots of clinking bangles.

'All righty. We need a bottle of boiled cooled water from the fridge.' She collected it on the way up to the bathroom.

'What's that for?' he asked.

'Washing his face—it's how Ally did it. She has what she calls a "top and tail" bowl.'

'A what?'

'To give him a quick wash instead of a bath. But you still use it for his face when you give him a bath.'

'Right.'

In the bathroom, she put the baby bath into the main bath. 'It's easier to use this than to put him in a big bath, because he can't sit up all on his own yet.'

'When will he do that?'

'When he's about six months old.'

Dylan looked at her, not sure whether to be impressed at her knowledge or annoyed by the one-upmanship. 'How come you know so much about babies?' Had she wanted a child of her own? he wondered. Were all women like Nadine, and just woke up one morning desperate for a baby?

'My bedtime reading,' she said lightly. 'I'll lend you the book, if you like—you'll probably find it useful.'

She undressed the baby, though Dylan noticed that she left Tyler's nappy on, and wrapped him in a towel. 'This is just to keep him warm while we're filling the bath. It needs to be lukewarm, and you need to put the cold water in first—it's better for it to be too cool, and for you to add a bit more warm water, than the other way round.' She demonstrated.

'How do you know when it's the right temperature?'

'You check the temperature of the water with
your elbow.' She dipped her elbow into the water.
'If it feels too warm, it'll be too hot for the baby.'

'Why don't you use that thermometer thing?'
He gestured to the gadget on the side of the bath.

She laughed. 'That was one of Pete's ideas.
You know how he loves gadgets.' Her smile
faded. 'Loved,' she corrected herself softly.

Awkwardly, Dylan patted her shoulder. 'Yeah.'

She shook herself. 'OK—now you pour the
cooled water into the bowl, dip a cotton wool pad
into it and squeeze it out, so it's damp enough
not to drag his skin but not so wet that water's
going to run into his eyes, then wipe his eyes.
You need to use a separate one for each eye; apparently that's to avoid infection.'

'Right.' He followed her instructions—which
were surprisingly clear and focused—and then
worried that he was being too clumsy, but the
baby didn't seem to mind.

'Now you wash his face and the creases round
his neck with a different cotton wool pad.'

When he'd finished doing that, she said, 'And

finally it's bath time.' She eyed his clothes. 'Sorry, I should've told you. Tyler likes to splash his hands in the bath, so you might get a bit wet.'

Dylan shrugged. 'It doesn't matter. This stuff will wash.'

She gave him an approving smile. It should've annoyed him that she was taking a position of superiority, but instead it made him feel warm inside. Which was weird. Emmy shouldn't make him feel warm inside. At all. He stuffed that into the box marked 'do not open' in his head, and concentrated on the task in hand.

'What about his hair?' he asked, looking at Tyler's soft fluffy curls.

'Do that before you put him in the bath,' she said. 'Keep him in the towel so he's warm, support his head with your hand and support him with your forearm—then you can scoop a little bit of water onto his hair and do the baby shampoo.'

Dylan felt really nervous, holding the baby—what if he dropped Tyler?—but Emmy seemed to have confidence in him and encouraged him as he gave Tyler a hair-wash for the very first time.

'Now you pat his hair dry. Be gentle and careful over the fontanelles.'

'Fontanelles?' he asked.

'Soft spots. The bones in his skull haven't completely fused, yet.'

That made Dylan feel even more nervous. Could he inadvertently hurt the baby? He knew he was making a bit of a mess of it, but she didn't comment.

'OK, now check the bath water again with your elbow.'

He dipped his elbow in. 'It feels fine.'

'Good. Now the nappy comes off, and he goes into the bath—support him like you did with the Humpty Dumpty thing.'

So far, so easy. Tyler seemed to enjoy the bath; as Emmy had warned him, there was a bit of splashing and chuckling.

Emmy stayed while he got the baby out of the bath and wrapped him in a towel with a hood to keep his head warm, then waited while Tyler did the nappy and dressed Dylan in a clean vest and Babygro.

She smiled at him. 'See, you're an expert now.'

Dylan didn't feel like it; but he was starting to

feel a lot more comfortable around Tyler, thanks to her. 'I'm trying, anyway.'

'I know you are—and that's all Tyler would ask for,' she said softly.

Dylan remembered how he'd thought she was trying in more than one sense; yet she wasn't judging him that way. He felt a bit guilty. 'I looked in the fridge. Is chicken stir-fry all right for dinner?'

'That'd be lovely, thanks.'

'Good. I'll call you when it's ready.'

'Are you OK about feeding him?' she asked. The doubts must have shown on his face, because she added, 'Just put the bottle of milk in a jug of hot water for a couple of minutes to warm up, then test it on the inside of your wrist to make sure it's warm but not hot.'

'How do you mean, test it on the inside of my wrist?'

'Just hold the bottle upside down and shake it over your wrist. A couple of drops will come out. If it feels hot then the milk's too hot.' She looked slightly anxious. 'Don't take this the wrong way—I'm not meaning to be patronising—but when you feed him you need to make sure the teat's full of milk, or he'll just suck in air.'

'Right.'

'And when you put him in his cot at bedtime, his feet need to be at the bottom of the cot so he doesn't end up wriggling totally under the covers and getting too hot.'

'OK,' he said, hoping he sounded more confident than he felt.

'Call me if you get stuck,' she said.

Which would be a cop-out. He could do this. It wasn't that hard to feed a baby, surely?

He managed to warm the milk, then sat down and settled the baby in the crook of his arm. Remembering what she'd said about the air, he made sure he tilted the bottle. The baby was very focused on drinking his milk, and Dylan couldn't help smiling at him. There was something really satisfying about feeding a baby, and he wished he'd been more involved earlier in the baby's life instead of backing off, fearing the extra intimacy.

This was what Nadine had wanted from him. What he hadn't been able to give, although now he was doing it for his best friend's child because he simply had no other choice. Except to walk away, which he couldn't bring himself to do.

He couldn't imagine Nadine doing this, even though he knew she'd wanted a baby of her own. She wouldn't have been comfortable exchanging her sharp business suits and designer dresses for jeans and a T-shirt. Dylan simply couldn't see her on the floor playing with a baby, or singing songs.

Unlike Emmy. Emmy, who'd been all soft and warm and cute...

He shook himself. He hadn't wanted children with Nadine. So her ultimatum of baby or divorce had given him an obvious choice. And he didn't want to think about his relationship with Emmy. Because, strictly speaking, it wasn't actually a relationship; it was a co-guardianship. They were here for Tyler, not for each other.

'Emotions and relationships,' he said softly to the baby, 'are very much overrated.'

When the baby had finished feeding, Dylan burped him in accordance with Emmy's instructions, then carried him up to the nursery and put him in his cot. There was a stack of books by the cot; Dylan found one in rhyme and read it through, keeping his voice soft and low. Tyler's eyelids seemed to be growing heavy; encouraged, Dylan read the next two books. And then finally Tyler's eyes closed.

Asleep.

Good. He'd managed it.

He touched the baby's soft little cheek. 'Sleep well,' he whispered.

Then he headed for the study and knocked on the open door.

Emmy looked up. 'How did you get on?'

'Fine. He's asleep. Dinner in ten minutes?'

'That'll be great. I'll just finish up here.'

She joined him in the kitchen just as he was serving up.

'OK if we eat in here, tonight?' Dylan asked.

'That's fine.' She took her first mouthful. 'This is very nice, thank you.'

He flapped a dismissive hand. 'It wasn't exactly hard—just stir-fry chicken, noodles, vegetables and soy sauce.'

'But it's edible and, more importantly, I didn't have to cook it. It's appreciated.'

There was an awkward silence for a few moments.

Work, Dylan thought. Work was always a safe topic. 'I saw that necklace you were making. I had no idea you made delicate stuff like that.'

'You mean you thought I just stuck some chunky beads on a string and that was it?' she asked.

He felt his face colour with embarrassment. 'Well, yes.'

She shrugged. 'There's nothing wrong with a string of chunky beads.'

He thought of his mother, and wanted to disagree.

'But no, I do mainly silverwork—and I also work with jet. I carve animals.'

'Like those ones on the shelf in Tyler's room?'

She nodded. 'Ally wanted a Noah's ark sort of thing, so I'd planned to do her one a month.'

'They're very good.'

'Thank you.' Emmy inclined her head at his compliment but he noticed that she accepted it easily. She clearly knew she was good at what she did. Just as he was good at what he did. Something they had in common, then.

'Why jet?' he asked.

'We always used to go to my great-aunt Syb's in the school summer holidays, up in Whitby.'

'Dracula country,' he said.

She smiled. 'Well, it's known for that nowadays, but it's also the Jurassic coastline, full of fossils—that's why there's lots of jet and amber in the cliffs there.'

'Amber being fossilised tree resin, right?'

She nodded. 'And jet's fossilised monkey puzzle tree. They used to use it a lot in Victorian times for mourning jewellery, but it's been used as jewellery for much longer than that. There are some Roman jewellery workshop remains in York, and archaeologists have found gorgeous jet pendants carved as Medusa's head.'

Dylan noticed how her eyes glittered; this was clearly something she felt really passionate about. For a second, it made him wonder what her face would look like in the throes of passion, but he pushed the thought away. It was way too inappropriate. He needed to keep his focus on work, not on how lush Emmy Jacobs' mouth was. 'And that's when you got interested in making jewellery, at your great-aunt's?'

She nodded. 'We used to go beachcombing

for jet and amber because Great-Aunt Syb's best friend Jamie was a jeweller and worked with it. I was fascinated at how these dull-looking, lightweight pebbles could suddenly become these amazingly shiny beads and flowers. Jamie taught me how to work with jet. It's a bit specialised.' She grimaced. 'I'd better warn you, it does tend to make quite a bit of dust, the really thick and heavy sort, but I always clean up after I've worked.'

If she'd said that a week ago, he would've scoffed; from what he'd seen, Emmy Jacobs was as chaotic as his mother. But now, having shared a house with her for a day and discovered that she ruled her life with lists and charts, he could believe it. She might appear chaotic, but she knew exactly what she was doing. 'How do you sell your jewellery? Do you have a shop?' He hadn't thought to ask before.

'No. I sell mainly through galleries—I pay them a commission when they sell a piece. Plus there's my website.'

'So what's the plan—to have a shop of your own?'

She shook her head. 'If I had a shop, I'd need

to increase production to cover all the extra expenses—rent, utilities and taxes, not to mention staffing costs. And I'd have to spend a lot of time serving customers instead of doing the bit of my job that I like doing most, creating jewellery. And then there's the worry about who'd cover the shop when an assistant was on holiday or off sick...' She grimaced. 'No, I'd rather keep it this way.'

She'd clearly thought it all through, taking a professional view of the situation, Dylan thought. He would never have expected that from her. And it shook him to realise how badly he'd misjudged her. He'd always thought himself such a good judge of character. How wrong he'd been.

'So what actually do you do?' she asked. 'I mean, Pete said you're a computer guru, but I assume you don't actually build computers or websites?'

He smiled. 'I can, and sometimes that's part of a project, but what I do is software development—bespoke stuff for businesses. So I talk to them about their requirements, draw up a specification, then do the architecture.'

'Architecture?' She looked puzzled.

'I write the code,' he said, 'so the computer program does what they want it to do. Once the code's written, you set up the system, test it, debug it, and agree a maintenance programme with the client.'

'So businesses can't just buy a software package—say like you do with word-processing, spreadsheets and accounting programs?'

'Obviously those ones they can, but what my clients tend to want is database management, something very specific to their business. So if they had a chain of shops, for example, they need to have the tills linked with the stock system, so every time they sell something it updates and they can see their stock levels. Once they get down to a certain stock level, it triggers a reorder report, based on how long it takes to get the stock from the supplier,' Dylan explained. 'It's also helpful if the till staff take the customer's details, because then they can build up a profile for the customer based on past purchases, and can use that knowledge to target their marketing more specifically.'

'Very impressive,' she said.

He shrugged. 'It's basic data management—

and it's only as good as the data you feed in. That's why the requirements and spec side is important. What the client thinks they want might not be what they actually want, so you have to grill them.'

'I can see you'd be good at that,' she said, then winced. 'Sorry, that was rude. I'm not trying hard enough.'

He should've been annoyed and wanting to snipe back; but he liked the fact that she was being honest. Plus he was beginning to suspect that she had quite a sharp wit, something he appreciated. 'It's OK. We've never really got on before, so we're not exactly going to be best friends, are we?'

'No, but we don't have to be rude to each other, either.'

'I guess not.' He paused. 'So do you use a computer system?'

'Sort of. I do my accounts on a spreadsheet because I'm a sole trader and don't need anything more complicated, but I did have my website designed so I could showcase my work and people could buy what they wanted online from me direct. It shows whether the piece they want is in stock or if they need to order it and how long it'll take—but, yes, I have to update that manually.'

Dylan made a mental note to look up her website. Maybe there was something he could add to it to make her life easier. Which didn't mean he was going soft; making things run smoothly for her meant that he wouldn't have to prop up their roster for more than his fair share of effort.

'So what's your big plan?' she asked. 'Expansion?'

'Pretty much keep doing what I do now,' he said. 'I have a good team. They're reliable and they're prepared to put in the hours to get the projects in on time.'

'And you like your job?'

'It's like breathing, for me,' he said honestly. Something that Nadine had never really quite understood. His job was who he was.

'Same here,' she said, surprising him. It was something else they had in common.

When they'd finished the meal, she said, 'It's my turn to do the dishes, and I'm not weaselling out of it—but there's something I need to share with you. Back in a tick.'

She returned with a book and handed it to him.

He read the title. '*The Baby Bible*. What's this?'

'You asked me how come I know so much about babies. It's because of this. I bought it when Ty was born, so I'd know what to do when Ally asked me to babysit. It tells you everything you need to know—how to do things, what all the milestones are.' She spread her hands. 'And if that doesn't work then I'll bring in my other secret weapon.'

'Which is?'

She looked slightly shame-faced. 'Ring my mum and ask her advice.'

He thought about what would happen if he rang his mother and asked for help with a baby. No, it wasn't going to happen. He was pretty sure his mother hadn't been able to cope with having a baby or a child, which was why she'd dumped him on her parents so many times. The only person he could've asked about babies was his grandmother, but she'd died a year ago now. After he'd married Nadine, but before the final split. And, although she'd never judged, never actually said anything about it, Dylan knew his grandmother had thought the wedding was a huge mistake.

How right she'd been.

What would she think about this set-up?

What would she have thought about Emmy?

He shook himself. 'Do you need it back soon?'

'I've read it through cover-to-cover once. But if you could leave it in Tyler's room or the kitchen when it's my shift, so I can refer to it if I need to, that'd be really helpful.' She glanced at her watch. 'Do you mind if I go back to work now and do the washing up later?'

'Sure—and I'm on nights tonight.'

'I would say sleep well, but...' She shrugged. 'That's entirely up to Tyler.'

'Yes.' And Dylan wasn't so sure he'd sleep well anyway. He still had to get his head round a lot of things. New responsibilities, having to share his space with someone else when he'd just got used to his bachelor lifestyle, and having a to-tally new routine for starters. Not to mention that getting to know Emmy was unsettling, because all his preconceptions about her were starting to look wrong. 'Sleep well,' he said, and went to settle down with his new reading material.

CHAPTER FIVE

THE BABY WOKE at half past three, and the wails coming through the baby listener seemed incredibly loud.

Dylan surfaced from some weird dream, switched off the baby listener and staggered out into Tyler's nursery.

According to what Emmy had told him—and what he'd read last night—screaming meant the baby was dirty, hungry, tired or wanted a cuddle. He picked the baby up and sniffed him. Nothing like yesterday's appalling whiff, so Tyler didn't need a nappy change. It was the middle of the night, so he could be tired—but then again, he wouldn't have woken if he was tired. So was he hungry, or did he just want a cuddle?

He probably wanted his mum. Though, Tyler was way too little to understand that Ally couldn't be there for him anymore. Not like Dylan's mother, who hadn't been there because she hadn't wanted to; Tyler had been very much loved by both his parents. And it was wrong, wrong, *wrong* that they'd died so young.

The baby nuzzled him.

Hadn't Emmy said that was a sign of hunger?

'OK, Ty, food it is,' he whispered. He took the baby down to the kitchen, managed to switch on the kettle and get the milk out of the fridge, and walked up and down with the baby, stroking his back to sooth him and jiggling him.

Dear God, why had nobody told him that babies were so *loud*? If Tyler carried on much longer, Emmy was bound to wake. And that wasn't fair because this was his shift, not hers, and he should be able to deal with this.

It seemed to take forever to heat the milk, and Tyler's wails grew louder and louder. Eventually Dylan managed it and tested the milk against his wrist. It wasn't as warm as yesterday, but hopefully it would be warm enough to keep the baby happy.

He sat in the dark while the baby guzzled his milk.

'Better now?' he asked softly. Not that he was going to get an answer.

Then he remembered about the burping thing. The last thing he wanted was for the baby to wake again, crying because his tummy hurt. Dylan felt like a zombie as it was. He held Tyler on his shoulder and rubbed the baby's back, then nearly dropped the baby when he heard a loud burp and felt an immediate gush of liquid over his bare shoulder. What? Why hadn't Emmy warned him about this? It hadn't happened last time. Had he done something wrong?

The baby began to cry again. Oh, hell—the burped-up milk had probably soaked his clothes, too, and he'd be cold. He needed a change of clothes; Dylan couldn't possibly put him back into his cot in this state.

Luckily the overhead light in the nursery was on a dimmer switch. Dylan kept it as low as possible, and hunted for clean clothes. Tyler seemed to have grown four extra arms and six extra legs, all of which were invisible, but eventually Dylan managed to get him out of the Babygro.

The nappy felt heavy; clearly that needed changing, too, before Dylan put clean clothes on the baby. But when he settled Tyler on the changing unit and opened the nappy, the baby promptly peed over him. Dylan jumped back in shock, then dashed forward in horror. This was his first night in charge and he was making a total mess of it. The baby could've rolled over and fallen off the changing station and been badly hurt.

His heart was hammering. Please, no. He'd already lost Pete and Ally; he couldn't bear the idea of anything happening to Tyler. Even though the baby had disrupted his life, even though it panicked him that he didn't know what he was doing, he was beginning to feel other emotions than just resentment towards Tyler.

He tried to make light of it, even though he was in a cold sweat. 'Help me out here, Ty,' he muttered. 'I'm new at all this.'

But finally the baby had a clean nappy and clean clothes. Dylan put him in the cot and made sure the covers were tucked in properly; within seconds Tyler had fallen back to sleep in his usual position with his arms up over his head, looking like a little frog.

Dylan went back to his room feeling almost

hung-over. It was way too late to have a shower; the noise from the water tank would wake Emmy. So he simply sponged off the worst of the milk at the sink in his en-suite, and fell into bed. How did parents of newborns cope with even less sleep than this? he wondered as he sank back into sleep. How had Pete not been a total zombie?

The next morning, his alarm shrilled at the usual time. Normally Dylan woke before his alarm, whereas today he felt groggy from lack of sleep. He staggered out of bed and showered; he didn't feel much better afterwards, though at least he didn't smell of burped-up milk anymore.

He went to the nursery to look in on Tyler. The baby was asleep in his cot, looking angelic. 'It's all right for some,' Dylan said wryly. 'I could do with a nap. So have an extra one for me.'

He dragged himself downstairs. Was it his imagination, or could he smell coffee?

Emmy was in the kitchen, sitting at the table with a mug of coffee. She raised an eyebrow when she saw him. 'Rough night?' she asked.

'Apart from Ty throwing up half the milk over me and then peeing over me...'

She burst out laughing and he glared at her. 'It's not funny.'

'Yes, it is.'

'You could've *warned* me he'd do that.'

She spread her hands. 'To be fair, he hasn't actually done that to me. But Ally told me he once did it to Pete.'

'Just don't tell me it's a male bonding thing,' he grumbled.

'And I thought you were supposed to be a morning person.' She laughed, and poured him a mug of coffee. 'Here. This might help.'

'Thanks. I think.' He took a sip. 'I was useless last night. I nearly let him fall off the changing station.'

She flapped a dismissive hand. 'I'm sure you didn't.'

'I jumped back from him when he peed on me.'

'Which is a natural reaction, and you would've been there to stop him if he'd started to roll.'

It still made him go cold, how close it had been. '*Can* he roll over?'

'Yes.' She rolled her eyes. 'Stop panicking, Dylan. You know what to expect now. You won't let him fall.'

How could she have so much confidence in him, when he had absolutely none in himself? And what had happened to her, anyway? The Emmy Jacobs he knew would've sniped about him not being good enough. This Emmy was surprisingly supportive. Which made him feel even more adrift. He was used to being in charge and knowing exactly what he was doing. Right now, he was winging it, and he hated feeling so useless.

He covered up his feelings by saying, 'I could do with some toast. Do we have bread?'

'Not much. But it's my turn for the supermarket run today, so I'll get some.'

'Right.'

'Any food allergies, or anything you hate eating?'

'No to the first, offal to the second.'

She smiled. 'That makes two of us. I'll pick up dinner while I'm out.'

He thought about it. Really, this was much like sharing a student house. Except it wasn't with his friends, it was with a near stranger. And he had the added responsibility of a baby. 'We need to sort out a kitty.'

'Sure. We can do that later.'

'And we need a rota for doing the shopping. Or maybe we could get the shopping delivered.' He frowned. 'Do you have a car?'

'Yes. And I know how to fit Ty's baby seat in it.' She paused. 'What about you?'

'Yes to having a car. I don't have a clue about a baby seat.'

'We only have one baby seat between us. I think we're going to need one for your car as well as mine.'

He frowned. 'So I need to take another afternoon off?'

She shrugged. 'Or we could go at the weekend.'

Her weekend on, his weekend off—and he was going to have to spend it doing baby stuff instead of catching up with work. Great. Yet more disruption. And then the guilt surged through him again. It wasn't Tyler's fault that he needed to be looked after—or that Dylan had agreed to do it. 'OK. We'll go at the weekend,' he said.

* * *

Saturday morning saw them in the nursery department of a department store in the city.

'Your baby's gorgeous,' the assistant said, cooing over Tyler.

Dylan was about to correct her when Emmy said, 'Yes, we think so.' She shot him a look, daring him to contradict her.

He thought about it. Strictly speaking, Tyler *was* their baby. Just not a baby they'd actually made together.

Then he wished he hadn't thought about making babies with Emmy. How soft her skin would be against his. How she smelled of some spicy, floral scent he couldn't quite place. How it made him want to touch her, taste her...

Oh, hell. He really couldn't have the hots for *Emmy*. He hadn't even looked at another woman since he'd split up with Nadine. Abstinence: that had to be what was wrong with him. That, or the fact that he'd done the night shift, the previous night, and Tyler had woken three times, so lack of sleep had fried his brain.

He shut up and let Emmy do the talking.

And then Emmy spied a cot toy, something

that apparently beamed pictures of stars and a moon on the ceiling and played a soft tinkling lullaby.

'Can we get this as well? I think he'd love it.'

'You mean, *you* love it.' Emmy seemed to like simple, childlike things. And Dylan hadn't quite worked out yet whether he found that more endearing or annoying. He certainly didn't loathe her as much as he once had. She was good with the baby, too.

Her eyes crinkled at the corners. 'OK, then, let's ask him.' She picked up the cot toy, crouched down beside the pram, switched it on and let Tyler see the lights and hear the lullaby.

Tyler's eyes went wide, then he laughed and held his hands out towards it.

Emmy looked up at him and smiled. 'I think that's a yes.'

Again a surge of attraction hit him. Was he crazy? This was Emmy Jacobs, who sparred with him and sniped at him and was his co-guardian. She was the last person he wanted to get involved with. But at the same time he had to acknowledge that there was something about her that really got under his skin. Something that made him want to know more about her. Get closer.

And that in itself was weird. He didn't do close. Never had. He didn't trust anyone to let them near enough—even, if he was honest with himself, Nadine.

The rest of the weekend turned out to be Dylan's first weekend of being a dad. Although it was officially Emmy's weekend on duty, he somehow ended up going to the park with her to take Tyler out for some fresh air. He noticed that she talked to Tyler all the time, even though there was no way a baby could possibly understand everything she said. She pointed out flowers and named the colours for him; she pointed out dogs and birds and squirrels.

She was clearly taking her duties as godmother and guardian really seriously, and Dylan was beginning to wonder just why he'd ever disliked her so much. Then again, this new Emmy didn't have a smart-aleck mouth. She didn't snipe, and she wasn't cynical and hard-bitten like the Emmy Jacobs he was used to.

Which one was the real Emmy? he wondered. Was she letting her guard down and letting him see the real her? Or was this just some kind of mirage and Spiky Emmy would return to drive him crazy?

They stopped at the café in the park, and Emmy asked for a jug of hot water to heat Tyler's milk. While she found them a table, he bought the coffees. He'd seen her looking longingly at the cinnamon pastries, so he bought her one of those as well.

'That's really kind of you,' she said when he brought the tray over to their table.

But her eyes were full of anguish. What was going on here? 'What's wrong?' he asked.

She sighed. 'I struggle with my weight. And no, that isn't your cue to tell me that I'm fine as I am. My job's pretty sedentary, so I only manage to keep my weight under control because I go to an exercise class three times a week. But things have changed, now, and I'm not going to have time for classes anymore. I haven't been since the week before Ally and Pete went to Venice.'

'You miss your classes?'

She shrugged. 'I'll manage.'

'That's not what I asked. You miss them?'

'Yes,' she admitted. 'It's ridiculously soon. But

yes, I miss them. I spend too much time sitting at my desk—I really lose track of time when I'm working—and the classes used to help me get the knots out and stretch my muscles.'

'When are they?'

'Mornings. Straight after the school run.' She shrugged. 'So when Ty's at school, in four years' time or so, I can go back to them.'

'Maybe,' he said, 'we can change our rota. I'll go in to the office a bit later, on the mornings when you have a class—though obviously that means I'll be back later on those days to make up the time.'

'You'd do that for me?' She looked startled, almost shocked; and then she gave him a heart-stopping smile. It was his turn to be shocked then, by how much her smile affected him. How it made him feel as if the room had just lit up. 'Thank you, Dylan. What about you—do you do anything you've had to give up and miss already?'

'The gym,' he admitted. 'It's my thinking time. And I kind of like the endorphin hit at the end.'

'Let me know when your sessions are, and we'll switch the rota round.' She looked at the pastry, then at him, and gave him another smile. 'Thank you, Dylan. That's so nice.'

'Pleasure,' he responded automatically. And he stifled the thought that actually, it was a pleasure, seeing her made happy by such a little thing.

He'd surprised himself, offering to change the rota so she could do her weekly classes. And she'd surprised him by immediately offering to do the same for him. Why had he ever thought her selfish, when she so obviously believed in fairness? Had he just read her wrong in the past, and it had snowballed to the point where it was easier to dislike her than to wonder if he'd got it wrong? Not wanting to think about his burgeoning feelings, he said, 'I've been talking to Pete's parents about the funeral. They'd like it to be in the same church where Pete and Ally got married.'

She nodded. 'Ally's parents said the same.'

'Good. It makes it easier that they agree.' He paused. 'But Pete's parents also said they want the wake at the house rather than in a hall somewhere.'

'So we'll have to cater it, you mean?'

He nodded.

She blew out a breath. 'Then I vote we get the local deli to do as much of it as possible, so all we have to do is lay stuff out on serving platters on the dining room table. And I'll rope my mum in to help. Between us we can manage the drinks.'

There was no point in asking his mother to help. Dylan couldn't remember whether she was in India or Bali, but he knew she was on retreat somewhere, and he also knew from experience that she wouldn't allow anything to interrupt that. Even if her only child really needed her help. He'd learned that one at a pretty early age. 'Right,' he said shortly.

She narrowed her eyes. 'Is everything OK, Dylan?'

'Yes.' He raked a hand through his hair. 'Just this whole thing...I still can't quite get my head around it. I still keep thinking Pete's going to walk through the door and ask us if we missed him.'

'Me, too,' she said. 'Ally's the first person really close to me I've lost. I guess it's a normal reaction, but I wonder when I'm going to stop missing her.'

'You don't stop missing her. You just get better at dealing with it.'

She said nothing, just looked at him. Those wide grey eyes were full of empathy rather than pity, so he found himself unexpectedly telling her the rest. 'My grandmother. She died last year. It's little things that catch you—a bit of music that reminds me of her, or walking past someone who's wearing the same perfume. Or seeing something in the shop that I know she'd love, and suddenly remembering that she's not going to be here for her birthday or Christmas so there's no point in buying it.'

She reached over and squeezed his hand. Just long enough to let him know that she understood and sympathised, but not long enough to be cloying. Weird. He hadn't expected to actually start *liking* Emmy.

He gave her the smallest, smallest smile. 'I'll talk to the vicar and sort that side of it out. The funeral directors just want a decision on the casket. Can I ask you to sort the food and drink?'

'Sure. Does anything else need doing?'

'I'm doing a eulogy for Pete. Do you want to do one for Ally?'

She shook her head. 'I don't think I could stand up there and do it. I would...' She paused, clearly swallowing back a sob. 'Well, I don't want to let her down by crying through it. She deserves more than that.'

He'd done enough presentations in his time to be able to get through it. 'I'll do it for you, if you like. Just tell me what you want to say and I'll read it out.'

She swallowed hard. 'Thank you.'

'No problem.'

'I could do a wall, though,' she said. 'I could scan in some of the photographs from when they were small, as well as the digital ones I've got from more recent years. We could talk to their parents and get their favourite memories as well.'

'That's a good idea. I'll talk to Pete's again while you talk to Ally's?'

'That works for me.'

'I think they'd like to stay at the house, that night,' Dylan said. 'I was thinking, it wouldn't be fair for either couple to stay in Pete and Ally's room.'

'You're right,' she agreed. 'It's my night on call, so I can use a sleeping bag in Tyler's room.'

'And I'll take the sofa,' he said.

Funny how their minds were in tune on this one.

Would they be in tune in other ways, too? The thought crept insidiously into his head and lodged there, and even though he tried to block it out he couldn't help being aware of just how attractive Emmy actually was.

She leaned down to touch the sleeping baby's cheek. 'You'll definitely know your mum and dad, Ty. Dylan and I, we have photographs and memories, all sorts of things we can share with you when you're older. Your mum did a "This Is Your Life" book for me when I was thirty, and I can do something like that for you of her.'

'I'll chip in with stuff about your dad,' he said, touching Tyler's other cheek.

They shared a glance and Dylan wondered— did it have to take the death of our best friends for us to get along? It was odd how easily they'd fallen into teamwork—since they'd moved into the house, he hadn't sniped once and neither had she—and he was shocked to realise that he actually liked her. A lot. Emmy was funny, clever, good company. How had he never noticed that before?

Emmy just about managed to get through the funeral, though she couldn't help bawling her eyes out during 'Abide With Me'. The bit about where was Death's sting always got to her. 'Amazing Grace' put a lump in her throat as well, and when the church echoed to Eva Cassidy singing 'Somewhere Over the Rainbow' there wasn't a dry eye anywhere.

Though she was glad that everyone was wearing bright colours rather than black, to celebrate Ally and Pete's life and the precious memories. It was important to share the good stuff as well as mourn them. To give them a decent send-off.

Tyler was an angel.

And Dylan was amazing.

He was sitting in the front row, next to her; when he stood up to do the eulogies from the pulpit, she couldn't take her eyes off him. Even though the tears were spilling down her cheeks as he spoke the words she'd written about her best friend.

She hugged him when he returned to his seat. 'You did a fantastic job,' she whispered. 'Just perfect.'

Dylan returned the hug, even though bits of him worried that he quite liked the feel of Emmy in his arms. He dismissed it simply as grief coming out. He *wasn't* attracted to Emmy Jacobs.

Ha—who was he trying to kid? Of course he was.

But he couldn't act on that attraction, for Tyler's sake. Getting involved with Emmy would make everything way too complicated. It would be better to keep his distance, the way he always did.

Friends neither he nor Emmy had seen since university days had come to the funeral. Back at the house, everyone was talking about the room divider Emmy had made with the photographs, sharing memories and the house echoed with as much laughter as tears.

The food was working out, too. Emmy was bustling around, sorting out the drinks and topping up the empty plates. Her mum had helped out and done way, way more than his own mother would've done if she'd been there. Between the three of them, they'd managed to handle this.

Finally everyone went and the clearing up started.

'You look really tired,' Emmy said gently to Ally's and Pete's parents. 'Why don't you go and lie down for a bit? Dylan and I can sort all this out.'

'We can't leave you to do all this, love,' Ally's dad said.

'Yes, you can. It's been a really tough day for us all, and I can't even begin to imagine how hard it's been for you. You need some rest. I'll bring you up a cup of tea in a minute.'

'Thank you, love,' Pete's mum said.

Again, Dylan found himself marvelling. Pete and Ally's parents clearly knew Emmy well and liked her. He was beginning to think that he was the one who was totally out of step. She'd been brilliant today. He made a mental note to cut her more slack in future.

Emmy's mum stayed to help, then kissed Emmy goodbye and, to Dylan's surprise, gave him a hug. 'Take care of yourself and call me if you need me, OK? That goes for both of you. Any time.'

He found himself envying Emmy's closeness to her mum. If only his own mother had been like that, maybe things would've been different. Maybe he would've known how to really love someone and not made such a mess of his marriage. Though he appreciated the way Emmy's mother had included him. How would Emmy have got on with his family? He had a feeling that Emmy would've liked his gran, and his gran would've liked Emmy.

And this was dangerous territory. He couldn't let himself think about this.

Emmy put Tyler to bed while he finished moving all the furniture back. Then she took a tray up to Pete and Ally's parents with tea and sandwiches.

When she came back down, Dylan noticed that she looked upset.

'Are you OK?' he asked.

She nodded. 'They're not coming down again today. I think it's exhausted all of them.' She bit her lip. 'It's so wrong, having to bury your child. It isn't the natural order of things. I really feel for them. Today they all seemed to age ten years in a matter of seconds. Did you see Ally's dad walking into church? He had to hold on to the side of the pew until he composed himself. It's not that long ago he was walking down that aisle with Ally on his arm in that gorgeous fish-tail dress, and you and Pete were waiting at the altar.'

'Yeah, I remember,' Dylan said softly. 'And you're right. Burying a parent must be hard, but it's more the natural order. Burying your child must be the worst feeling in the world.'

'And there's nothing we can do to make it better.' Her voice cracked and she looked anguished.

'I know, but I think we did Pete and Ally proud,' he said. 'Everyone was here celebrating them.'

She nodded. 'You're right. I think it's what they would've wanted.'

He wandered over to look at the photos on the divider, and saw the one of Emmy and Ally together as students.

'Your hair looks absolutely terrible. Whatever made you dye it blue?'

She came to join him and shrugged. 'I was a design student. We all did that sort of thing back then.'

'It looks nice now. Obviously it's not your natural colour but it suits you. It brings out your eyes.' He reached out to brush a lock of hair from her face.

'Careful, Dylan. Anyone might think we were on the way to being friends, with you paying me compliments like that.'

He raised an eyebrow. 'Maybe we are.'

She dragged in a breath. 'I wish it hadn't taken Ally and Pete to die before we started to see— well, what *they* saw in us.'

'Me, too.' He gave her a crooked smile. 'We can't change the past. But, for what it's worth, I'm sorry I misjudged you. You're not the needy, flaky mess I thought you were.'

Her eyes filled with tears. 'I'm sorry I misjudged you, too. You're still a bit judgemental, and you open your mouth before you think about what's going to come out of it. You might have the social skills of a rhino, but you do have a heart.'

Did he? Sometimes he wasn't so sure. He'd built so many walls around it that it was lost.

She rubbed her eyes with the back of her hand. 'Now I'm being wet. Ignore me.'

'It's OK. I'm not that far off crying, myself,' he admitted. He looked at her. 'Do you want a glass of wine?

She nodded.

'Me, too. Come on.'

He poured them each a glass of wine and then put some soft piano music on before curling up on the opposite end of the sofa to her. Her toes touched his ankle, but it didn't make him want to pull away. Weirdly, he felt more comfortable with her now, on one of the saddest days of his life, than he ever had before.

'I like this. What is it?' she asked.

'Einaudi. You work to classical music, don't you?'

'Vivaldi—not "the Four Seasons", because that's been overplayed to the point where I find it almost impossible to listen to it, but I like his cello concerti. They're calming and regular, good to work to.'

'I was looking at your website,' he said. 'You're very talented.'

She looked surprised, but inclined her head in acknowledgement of the compliment. 'Thank you.'

'But you could really do with a proper stock management program. I've written one and tested it for you. Let me know your admin password, and I'll install it for you.'

Her eyes widened. 'You've written me a program?'

'It's only a simple one.' He flapped a dismissive hand. 'It's pretty intuitive, so it won't take you five minutes to get to grips with it.'

'You've actually written me a program.' Tears glittered in her eyes.

He shrugged, feeling awkward. 'It's no big deal, Emmy. It wasn't that time-consuming.'

'But you still made the time to do it. Which is amazing, especially as we've both got all these new responsibilities and we're adjusting to all the changes in our lives.' She dragged in a breath. 'Thank you, Dylan.'

'It was entirely selfish of me,' he said. 'If it makes your life easier, then our rota will run more smoothly.'

She gave him a look that told him she didn't believe a word of it. That she knew he'd done it partly because he'd wanted to do something nice for her, even though there was no way he'd ever admit that out loud. 'Even so. Thank you.' She bit her lip. 'I just wish it hadn't taken—well, *this*, to get us in any kind of accord.'

'Me, too. But we've cracked the first week and a half. We're both there for Tyler. We'll make this work,' he said. And he meant every single word.

CHAPTER SIX

OVER THE NEXT few weeks, Emmy and Dylan settled in to their new routine. They shared Tyler's care during the week; Emmy had found a Pilates class nearby, which was scheduled at a similar time to her old class, and Dylan had found a gym nearby, too. And Emmy was surprised at how quickly she'd got used to the routine of working and family life.

'You know, Ty, I never thought it would end up being like this,' she said, jiggling the baby on her lap. 'I thought he'd be a nightmare to share a house with. Fussy and demanding and annoying. But he's actually OK, when you get to know him. He still has the social skills of a rhino, but I think that's because nobody taught him, not because he's too arrogant to care.'

Tyler cooed at her.

She laughed. 'He's better with you, too. I've heard him reading to you. Funny, he said he never wanted to be a dad, but he's managing just fine with you.' Her smile faded. 'I can't quite work him out. Why was he so adamant that he didn't want kids? And why did his marriage break up?'

She jiggled Tyler still further. 'Before we became your guardians, I would've said that Dylan was the problem. Nobody could put up with someone who's that formal and stuffy.' She frowned. 'Except that's not what he's really like. Now we've managed to reach a truce, I think I actually like him. He's got a dry sense of humour, and that smile...'

No. She wasn't going to allow herself to think about his smile and how it made her feel. She needed to keep her head where Dylan Harper was concerned, and keep this strictly—well, not business, exactly, but co-guardianship meant being professional and letting her head rule her heart. Total common sense.

She couldn't ask Dylan why he didn't want kids or why his marriage had fallen apart, because she knew it would annoy him. Dylan didn't like emotional stuff. Even if she did manage to push past that particular boundary, he was intensely private and she knew he'd give little away.

'I guess I'm going to have to learn not to ask,' she said, and Tyler gave her a solemn look as if he agreed.

The baby had started sleeping through the night again; clearly he was beginning to settle after the huge upheaval in his life. But when he began to wake two or three times in the night again, Emmy was at her wits' end.

'Lavender oil?' Dylan asked when she suggested it as a solution.

'A couple of drops on a hankie in his room. Apparently it's relaxing.'

'That's so flaky,' Dylan said. 'There's no scientific proof that it works.'

'I don't care. It's worth a try.' When he continued to look sceptical, she said, 'We have to do *something*, Dylan. I mean, I know we're taking alternate nights to go in to him—but when he wakes up, he's yelling loudly enough to wake whoever's not on duty.'

'I guess so.'

'I don't know about you, but I feel like a zombie.' She couldn't help yawning.

'Me, too,' he admitted. 'OK. Try the lavender oil.'

But it didn't work.

The next day, Emmy made an appointment with the health visitor. 'We might have a solution,' she told Dylan when he came home. 'Ally's health visitor says either he's starting to cut teeth, or he's ready to start solid food.'

'So what do we do now? Buy jars of stuff?' Dylan asked.

Emmy shook her head. 'We start with baby rice and mix it with his milk—so then the taste is quite near what he's used to.' She produced a packet of organic baby rice she'd bought at the supermarket on the way home from seeing the health visitor. 'So let's do this.'

Dylan read out the instructions from the back of the packet, and Emmy followed them.

'It doesn't look much,' Dylan said doubtfully. 'Are you sure you measured out the right amount?'

'I did what you read out,' she said, and sat down with Tyler. She put a tiny amount of the rice on the end of the spoon. 'Come on, sweetie, just one little mouthful,' she coaxed, and put the spoon into Tyler's open mouth.

The result was baby rice spattered all over her.

Dylan smothered a laugh. 'Sorry. But…'

'I look ridiculous. I know.'

'Let me see if I can persuade him to try it,' Dylan suggested.

But he got nowhere, either.

He looked at Emmy. 'So, Ally didn't do any of this with him?'

Emmy thought about it. 'She did talk about weaning him. She said she was planning to start—' she gulped '—when she got back from Venice.'

But that moment was never to happen.

Dylan patted her shoulder briefly in sympathy, then grabbed a paper towel, wetted it under the tap, and wiped the spattered baby rice from her face.

She gave him a wry smile. 'I'm glad you used water on that paper towel before you wiped my face.'

'A dry towel wouldn't have got it off.'

'That's not what I meant.'

He frowned. 'I'm not with you.'

'I mean, I'm glad that you used water and not spit.'

She saw the second the penny dropped. 'That's really *gross*!' But he laughed.

'It's what my mum used to do,' she said with a grin. 'Didn't yours?'

'No.' His tone was short and his smile faded.

What was Dylan's issue with his mum? Emmy wondered. Was he not close to her? Was that why he kept people at a distance?

He switched the subject by tasting the rice. 'I think I know why he's spitting it out.'

'Why?'

'Try it.'

She did. 'It's tasteless. Bland.' She grimaced. 'But I guess it's about getting him used to texture rather than taste.'

'So we'll have to keep going.'

They muddled through the next few days, and finally Emmy cheered. 'Yay! He's actually eating it.'

She put up a hand to high-five Dylan. He

paused—but then he surprised her by high-fiving her. 'Result.'

'*The Baby Bible* says we should introduce one new food at a time, leaving three or four days in between, so we can spot any food allergies,' Emmy said later that evening. 'They say it's good to start with carrots—so I'll steam some and purée them for him tomorrow night.'

The carrots went down as badly as the baby rice had the previous week.

'It's a new taste. It took a couple of days with the baby rice, so we'll have to just persevere,' Dylan said. He scooped Tyler out of his high chair. 'And I will clean up this little one while you, um…' His eyes crinkled at the corners. 'While you de-carrot yourself.'

'I am *so* wearing an apron, next time I try and get him to eat solids,' Emmy said. 'Thanks. I need to change.'

But when she came out of the bedroom, she saw Dylan coming out of the bathroom wearing just his jeans and no shirt, with the baby cradled in his arms.

'Did you get splashed?' she asked.

'Just a bit.' He grinned at her.

Oh, help. Her mouth had gone dry. She knew he went to the gym regularly, but she'd had no idea how perfect his musculature was. That he had a six-pack and well-shaped arms.

And she really hadn't expected to feel this surge of attraction to a man who'd always been prickly and standoffish with her, and sometimes downright rude.

Then again, she had a rubbish choice in men. She'd picked loser after loser who'd let her down and made her feel like the most unattractive woman in the universe. OK, Dylan wasn't a loser, and he wasn't the stuffy killjoy she'd also thought him; but he was the last person she could get into a relationship with. Her relationships never lasted, and Tyler would be the one who paid the price when it all went wrong. She couldn't do that to the baby, especially as he'd already lost so much. So instead she made a light, anodyne comment, let Dylan put Tyler to bed, and fled to the safety of her workbench. Working on an intricate piece would take all of her mental energy, and she wouldn't have enough space left to think about Dylan. To dream about something that just couldn't happen.

* * *

The next night, Tyler woke an hour after she put him to bed, and started crying.

She groaned. 'I'm rubbish at this parenting business. He's never going to sleep again.'

Dylan followed her up to his room. 'The book said babies cry because they need a nappy change, they're hungry, they're tired, they're bored, or they want a cuddle.'

'I've fed him, and he's had more solids today, so I don't think he's hungry. He's clean and dry, so it's not that. I don't think he's bored. But this isn't the same cry as when he's tired or wants a cuddle.' She bit her lip. 'I think I might need to call Mum.'

'Wait a second. Do you think he's teething?' Dylan asked. 'Didn't the health visitor say something about that?'

Emmy frowned. 'His face is red, so he might be. Give him a cuddle for a second, will you, while I wash my hands? Then I can check his mouth.'

Dylan held the baby until she came back with clean hands. She put her finger into Tyler's mouth and rubbed it gently over his gums. 'I can't feel anything—but, ow, his jaws are strong.'

Tyler was still crying.

'What are we going to do, Dylan?'

He grimaced. 'I was reading something the other day about you have to let them lie there and cry so they get used to falling asleep on their own.'

She shook her head. 'I hate that idea. He's upset about something or he wouldn't be crying.'

'Let me try something.' Dylan rocked the baby and seemed to be talking to him, but his voice was so soft that Emmy couldn't quite catch what Dylan was saying. But the amazing thing was that the baby actually settled and went back to sleep.

Dylan put him down gently in the cot, and Tyler started crying again.

'What did you do before?' Emmy asked.

He flushed. 'I sang to him.'

Emmy was surprised; she hadn't thought Dylan was the type to sing. 'Do it again—but don't pick him up, because maybe it was putting him back down that woke him.'

Dylan shrugged, and sang 'Summertime' in a rich baritone.

And she was mesmerised. OK, so she'd heard

him sing in church at the funeral, but she'd been preoccupied then. She'd had no idea he could sing like this. Like melted chocolate, rich and smooth and incredibly...

She stopped herself. Not sexy. It would be a bad move to think of that word in conjunction with Dylan Harper.

The baby yawned, and finally his hands flopped down and his eyes closed.

Dylan stopped singing and leaned over the edge of the cot. 'How can they sleep like that? He looks a bit like a frog—and I'm sure that can't be comfortable.'

'It's probably a lot more comfortable than it looks, or he'd lie in a different position,' she pointed out. 'I think he looks cute.' She shared a glance with Dylan. 'You have a good voice, Dylan.'

He raised an eyebrow. 'Was that grudging or surprised?'

'Surprised,' she admitted. 'I didn't think you'd—well, be a singer. Or know a song like that.'

'My grandmother used to sing it to me when I was little.'

She smiled. 'It's a beautiful song.'

'Yes.' And it was weird how much that compliment from her had warmed him. Nobody had ever commented on his singing before. Then again, he'd never really sung in front of anyone, except in church at a wedding or christening. His throat tightened: *or at a funeral*. 'We'd better leave him to sleep,' he said gruffly, and left the room abruptly before he did anything stupid, like asking Emmy to spend time with him. They were co-guardians, and that was all.

A couple of days later, Dylan came home early to find Emmy in tears. His stomach clenched. What was wrong?

'Is something wrong with Tyler?' he asked.

She shook her head. 'I would've called you if there was a problem.'

'What's the matter?'

'I just—' she gulped '—I just miss Ally. Tyler…She's missing out on all his firsts. He's getting his first tooth—you can actually see a little bit of white on the edge of his gums now.'

'That must be why he was crying the other night.'

She nodded. 'And he said "dada" today.' She dragged in a breath. 'Ally would've called me to talk about all this. And I'm the one seeing it, when it should be her, and I can't even talk to her about it. This is all so *wrong.*'

Tears would normally send Dylan running a mile. He'd hated it when Nadine cried. He'd always found an excuse to back away. But he couldn't just walk away and leave Emmy distressed like this.

'I miss them, too,' he said, and wrapped his arms round her.

Big mistake.

She was warm and soft in his arms. Her hair smelled of spring flowers, and felt like silk against his cheek, smooth and soft and shiny.

Emmy froze. This was bad. Dylan was holding her. And she was holding him right back.

Comfort. This was all this was, she told herself.

But then she pulled back and looked up at him.

His eyes were a dark, stormy blue.

And his mouth—since when had Dylan had such a lush mouth? She wasn't sure whether she wanted to stroke it first, or kiss it, or what. Just that she wanted him.

She glanced back up to his eyes and realised he was staring at her mouth, too.

No. *No.* This was a seriously bad idea.

But her mouth was already parting, her head tipping back slightly in offering.

His mouth was parting, too.

And slowly—oh, so slowly—he lowered his head to hers. His mouth skimmed against hers, the touch as light as a butterfly's wing. It wasn't enough. It wasn't anywhere near enough. She wanted more. Needed more.

Even though her common sense was screaming at her to stop, her libido was doing the equivalent of sticking fingers in ears and saying, 'La, la, la, I can't hear you.' And she found herself reaching up on tiptoe to kiss him back, her lips brushing against his. It was like some kind of exquisite torture; close, yet not close enough.

His arms tightened round her, and then he was really kissing her. His mouth moved against hers, tentative and unsure at first, then more demanding. And she was kissing him all the way back, matching him touch for touch.

She'd never, ever felt like this before. Even the guy she'd once thought she'd end up marrying hadn't made her feel like this when he kissed her. What on earth was going on?

Dylan untucked her shirt from the waistband of her jeans and slid his fingers underneath the cotton, splaying his palms against her back. He moved his fingertips in tiny circles against her skin; his touch aroused her still more, near to fever pitch.

If he asked her, she knew she'd go to bed with him right now and to hell with the consequences. She wanted Dylan more than she'd ever wanted anyone in her entire life.

She made a tiny sound of longing, and he stopped.

He looked utterly shocked. His mouth was reddened and swollen, and she was pretty sure hers was in the same state.

This was bad. Really bad.

'Emmy, we—I—' He looked dazed.

'I know. We shouldn't have done this,' she said quickly, and pulled away from him. She needed to do some serious damage limitation, and fast. 'Let's pretend this didn't happen. I was upset and you were comforting me, and you're missing Ally and Pete as much as I am, and it just got a bit out of hand.'

His face was suddenly inscrutable. 'Yes, you're right. It didn't happen.'

'I—um—I'd better start making dinner. I'm running a bit late. Sorry, I know you hate it when things aren't on time.' Flustered, she rushed out to the kitchen before he could say anything else. She really didn't want to humiliate herself any further.

Dylan watched her go, not stopping her. Oh, help. He really shouldn't have kissed her like that. Now he knew what Emmy tasted like, it was going to haunt his dreams.

But he knew she was right. They couldn't do this. It would make things way too complicated because of Tyler.

They'd just have to be firmer with themselves in future. A lot firmer.

CHAPTER SEVEN

EMMY PUT THE phone down, beaming and hugging herself. She wanted to leap up and cheer and do a mad dance all through the house, but she knew she couldn't or else she'd wake the baby.

This was the best promotional opportunity she'd ever been offered. It could lead to a real expansion of her business; and it could be the making of her name.

Her smile faded as she thought about it. The deadline was tight. She was going to have to work crazy hours to get the pieces made on time. Which meant that she was going to have to ask Dylan to help her out.

And things had been awkward between them since—well, since she'd wept all over him and he'd held her and they'd ended up kissing. He'd kept out of her way as much as possible, and they only stayed in each other's company for as long as it took to update each other about Tyler or to eat dinner. And dinner meant no talking, because Dylan had retreated into reading journals at the table. It was horribly rude and she knew he knew it; but it was an excuse to avoid her, and there was nothing she could do about it.

They'd agreed early on that they'd work as a team and support each other when they needed it. But had their kiss cancelled out that agreement?

Maybe if she made something really special for dinner, it would knock Dylan off balance and he'd talk to her. And then she could ask him.

She browsed through Ally's cookery books and found a fabulous recipe for monkfish wrapped in parma ham. It seemed pretty simple to cook but it looked really swish. That would have to do the trick, surely? She made a list of what she needed and took Tyler out in his pram to the parade of shops round the corner. After the fishmonger's, she went to the deli, the baker's and the greengrocer's.

She chatted to the baby on the way. 'This could

be my big career break. Clap your hands and wish Aunty Emmy good luck, Ty.'

Tyler clapped his hands and giggled. She laughed back at him. 'You're just gorgeous— you know that?'

So was Dylan.

And she wasn't supposed to be thinking about that.

She played with the baby when they got home; both of them thoroughly enjoyed the bubble-blowing. Tyler was grabbing toys now and rattling them. It was amazing how a little one could take over your life like this. Emmy could see entirely why Ally hadn't wanted to go back to the job she'd once loved, not once Tyler was around.

Then her phone beeped. She checked it to find a text message from Dylan. *Sorry, emergency project meeting. Will be late home. Let me know if problem.*

Normally, Emmy would've been a bit cross at the late notice of a rota change; but today she was relieved, as it would mean that Dylan would come home feeling slightly in her debt and he might be more amenable to what she wanted to ask.

And then she felt horrible and manipulative. That really wasn't fair of her. It was an emergency meeting, after all, so he must be up to his eyes.

She fed Tyler some puréed apple—his food repertoire was expanding beautifully now—then gave him a bath, not minding that he kept banging his toy duck into the foamy water and splashing her. She put him to bed, sang to him and put his light show on, then changed into dry clothes and headed downstairs to the kitchen.

There was another text from Dylan on her phone. *On way now. Sorry.*

Oh, help. He'd be here before dinner was ready, at this rate.

She prepared the monkfish hastily and put it in the oven, then finished laying the table in the dining room.

Dylan walked in holding a bouquet of bright pink gerberas and deep blue irises, the kind of flowers she loved and bought herself as an occasional treat. 'For you,' he said, and handed it to her.

She stared at him, surprised. Why on earth would Dylan buy her flowers? It wasn't her birthday, and they weren't in the kind of relationship where he'd buy her flowers. 'Thank you. They're, um, lovely.'

'But?'

Obviously it was written all over her face. She gave him a rueful smile. 'I was just wondering why you'd bought me flowers.'

'Because I'm feeling guilty about being late,' he said.

Even if he said no to helping her, at least this late meeting had thawed the ice between them. And she was grateful for that.

'I bought them from the supermarket on the way home from the office. Sorry I'm late,' he said again.

'It's not a problem. You gave me as much notice as you could. Come and sit down in the dining room; dinner's almost ready. You've obviously had a tough day.'

'You could say that.' He didn't elaborate, and Emmy wasn't sure enough of herself to push him.

She poured him a glass of wine, then served dinner.

He frowned. 'This is a bit posh. And we normally eat in the kitchen. Is it some sort of special occasion? Your birthday?'

'No-o,' she hedged. 'I just wanted to make a bit of an effort, that was all.'

Except the second she took her first mouthful she realised that something had gone wrong. Really, *really* wrong. Instead of the nice, tender fish she'd expected, it was rubbery and tough, and the potato cakes she'd made were a bit too crisp at the edges.

'Oh, no—I'm sure I followed the recipe to the letter. I must've had the oven up too high or something.'

But Dylan didn't look annoyed, just rueful. 'Well, it *looked* nice.'

'And it tastes vile.' She grimaced. 'I'm so sorry.'

'Don't worry. Tell you what—get rid of this, and I'll order us pizza.' He took his mobile phone out of his pocket and tapped in a number.

She took their plates to the kitchen and scraped the food into the bin. Right then, she wanted to burst into tears. She'd ruined dinner. How could she ask him a favour now?

'Hey, it could easily have happened when I was

cooking. Don't worry about it,' he said, coming into the kitchen to join her.

She wasn't worried about the *food*.

When she didn't reply, he rested a hand on her shoulder. 'Emmy, what's wrong?'

She took a deep breath. 'I was going to ask you a favour. I can't now.'

'Why not?'

'Because, instead of giving you a decent dinner, I served you something disgusting.'

He waved a dismissive hand. 'It's not a problem, Emmy—though maybe in future it might be an idea to stick to stuff you actually know how to cook?'

'I guess so,' she said ruefully.

'So what did you want to ask me?'

She squirmed. 'There isn't an easy way to ask.'

'Straight out will do.'

'I got a call from one of the big glossy magazines. They want to do a feature on up-and-coming British jewellery designers and they want to interview me.'

'That's good, isn't it?' he asked.

'Ye-es.'

'But?'

She sighed. 'But they want me to make some jewellery and their deadline's massively tight. My guess is that someone dropped out at the last minute and I was a second choice, and I think there are another two designers they've asked as well, so there's no guarantee I'll be included anyway.'

'But they still asked you, and that's the main thing. How tight is the deadline?'

This was the deal-breaker, she knew. 'They've asked me to create something totally new for them. So I need to spend the next four days working solidly to get the pieces made on time for their shoot.'

'So you need me to take over Tyler's care for the next four days?'

She nodded. 'But you had an emergency project meeting tonight, so you're clearly up to your eyes and it's not doable.'

'I can delegate.'

'I'll just have to pass and ask if they'd consider me in the future. If I tell them about Ty, maybe then they'll be understanding and won't think I'm too lazy and just making up feeble excuses.'

He placed a finger over her mouth, making her skin tingle. 'Emmy, were you listening? I said I'd do it. I'll delegate.'

Her eyes went huge. 'Really?'

'Really,' he said softly.

Then he dropped his hand, before he did anything stupid—like moving it to cup her cheek and dip his head to kiss her. That kiss was still causing him to wake up at stupid o'clock in the morning and wonder what would happen if he did it again. He needed to keep a lid on his attraction towards Emmy. Now.

'Thank you,' she said. 'I—well, I feel bad about asking. Four days is a lot.'

'This is your big break, Emmy. And we're a team. Of course I'll do it.'

'Thank you.'

He couldn't resist teasing her. 'I will be exacting repayment, of course.'

Then he wished he hadn't said it when she blushed. Because now all sorts of things were running through his head, and none of them were sensible. All of them involved Emmy naked in his bed. Which would be a very, very bad idea for both of them. Hadn't he spent the last week or so trying to get his feelings under control and forcing himself to think of her as just his co-guardian?

'I mean, I want four days off in lieu,' he said.

She dragged in a shaky breath, and he had the feeling that her thoughts had been travelling along very similar lines to his own. 'That's a deal,' she said.

The doorbell rang, and the pizza delivery boy saved him from saying anything else stupid—such as suggesting they sealed the deal with a kiss. He made sure they had the full width of the kitchen table between them when they sat down to eat. Maybe, just maybe, his common sense would come back and do its usual job once he'd eaten. He needed carbs.

Sharing a house with a woman he knew he shouldn't be attracted to was turning out to be much harder than he'd expected. Though he knew that at least work was a safe topic. 'Tell me about the magazine,' he invited.

'It's one of the biggest women's monthly magazines, glossy and aspirational stuff.' She smiled.

'It's not exactly the kind of thing you'd be likely to read.'

No, but he knew the kind of thing that Nadine had flicked through and he had a pretty good idea of what they required.

'And they're featuring your work?'

'*If* they like it. There aren't any guarantees,' she warned. 'As I said, there are a couple of other designers in the running.'

'They'll like your work,' he said. 'What do they want you to make?'

'A pendant, rings, earrings, and a bangle— they want an ultra-modern set and an ultra-girly, almost old-fashioned set.'

'Like that filigree stuff you do.'

She nodded. 'Exactly that.'

A pendant, rings, earrings and a bangle. And his imagination *would* have to supply a vision of Emmy wearing said jewellery, and nothing but said jewellery.

'Are you going to show them your jet animals as well?' he asked, pushing the recalcitrant thoughts away.

She wrinkled her nose. 'No, they're just a bit of fun.'

'But they're different, Emmy. People might forget your name if they want to buy your jewellery, but they'll definitely remember your jet animals, so they'll look them up on the Internet and find you.'

She thought about it. 'Fair point.'

'Go for it,' he said. 'Maybe that little turtle you made for Ty last week. And the dolphin.'

'I could do a seahorse,' she said, seeming to warm to the idea.

'That would definitely do it,' he said. 'A jet seahorse.'

'I owe you,' she said, finishing her pizza. 'Would you mind…?'

'Go. You're off housework, childcare and everything else,' he said. 'Go beat that deadline.'

She went off to work, and he made a phone call to delegate his work for the next four days so he could take over from her. It was a lot to ask, but he also knew that if he'd been the one to ask the favour her reaction would've been the same: total support. And he could give her some help to chase her dream.

Over the next four days, Emmy worked crazy hours to get the pieces done—a solid jet heart with silver filigree radiating out into a larger heart-shaped pendant, matching earrings, and delicate filigree cuffs containing the shape of a heart in solid jet. The other set included a modern pendant of a jet cone with a slice of amber running through it, matching earrings, a jet ring that entwined with an amber one, and a bangle that replicated the same effect, a thin band of amber entwined with a thin band of jet. And to finish the collection she carved the jet seahorse she'd discussed with Dylan.

Outside her work, she didn't have time to do anything other than have a quick shower in the morning, then fall into bed exhausted at night. Dylan brought her coffee and fruit and sandwiches to keep her going during the day, but didn't stay long enough to disturb her. He did insist on her taking a short break in the evening, though, to eat a proper dinner. She gave him a grateful smile. 'Thank you, Dylan. You've been a real star.'

'You'd do the same for me. How's it going?'

'I'm getting there.'

When she'd finished, she showed him the two collections.

'This is beautiful. I know a lot of women who'd love something like this.' He smiled at her. 'You're definitely going to get this.'

'There are no guarantees,' she reminded him.

Emmy delivered the jewellery to the magazine offices by hand, including the jet seahorse. She knew she was being paranoid, but she couldn't trust them to anyone else. She'd put too much of her heart and soul into the project now for things to go wrong.

Then it was a matter of waiting.

Were they going to choose her?

And how long would they keep her waiting before they delivered the verdict?

Every second seemed to drag—even though she knew she was being ridiculous and she probably wouldn't hear for at least a week. But by the time she got back to the house in Islington, she felt flat.

Dylan took one look at her. 'Right. We're going out.'

'Where?' she asked.

'You need some fresh air, and Ty and I are going with you to keep you company—isn't that right, sweetheart?' he added to the baby. 'I've got his bag organised. All I need to do is get a couple of bottles from the fridge, and we're good to go.'

She gave in. 'Thank you, Dylan.'

'I know you like the sea,' he said as he finished packing the baby's bag. 'And I think it's what you need to blow the cobwebs out.'

'But it's nearly five hours from here to Whitby,' she blurted out.

He laughed. 'I know. I'm not taking you there. I thought we could go to Sussex.'

In the end he drove them to Brighton, where they crunched over the pebbles next to the sea. Part of Emmy was wistful for the fine, soft sand of the east coast she was used to, but she was seriously grateful that Dylan had thought of it. 'You're right. The sea's just what I need. Thank you so much.'

'My pleasure.' He smiled at her, and her heart did a flip. Which was totally ridiculous.

They ate fish and chips on the pier. He fed little bits of fish to Tyler, who absolutely loved it and opened his mouth for more.

'I think we've just found the next food for his list,' Dylan said with a grin.

The woman sitting on the bench next to them looked over. 'Oh, your baby's just adorable.'

Emmy froze.

But Dylan simply smiled. 'Thank you. We think so, too.'

For a moment Emmy wondered what it would be like if this were real—if Dylan were her partner and Tyler were their baby. Then she reminded herself that they were co-guardians. They'd agreed that kiss was a mistake. She'd be stupid to want more than she could have.

'You're quiet,' Dylan remarked when they were wandering through the narrow streets of boutique shops, with Tyler fast asleep in his pushchair.

'I'm just a bit tired,' she prevaricated.

'And worrying about whether they're going to like your designs?'

She frowned. 'How did you know?'

'I'm the same whenever I bid for a project. I always know I've done my best, but I always worry whether the client will like what I've suggested.'

'And I guess you have the added pressure, because you have people relying on you for work.'

He shrugged. 'There is that.'

She grimaced. 'Sorry, that was patronising and a stupid thing to say.'

'It's OK. You've done the equivalent of a week and a half's normal office hours over four days. I'm not surprised your brain is a bit fried. Come on. Let's get an ice cream.'

'Good idea. And it's my shout.'

Emmy fell asleep in the car on the way back. Dylan glanced at her.

Now he understood exactly what Nadine had meant. The idea of having a partner and a child to complete his life. He hadn't understood it at the time. After his own experiences of growing up, he'd sworn never to have a child of his own. Even to the point where he'd split up from the woman he'd loved rather than have a child with her.

And yet here he was in exactly that position: a stand-in father to Tyler. Something he hadn't wanted to do, but guilt and duty had pushed him into it. He wasn't sure what surprised him more, the fact that he was actually capable of looking after the baby and giving him the love he needed, or the fact that he was actually *enjoying* it. Part of him felt guilty about that, too. He hadn't given Nadine that chance. Maybe if she'd forced his hand, stopped taking the Pill without telling him and just confronted him with the news that he was going to be a dad, he would've got used to the idea. She'd played fair with him by giving him the chance to say no; and he'd been stubborn enough and selfish enough to say exactly that.

On paper, Nadine had been the perfect choice: focused, career-orientated, organised. Just as he was. Except it hadn't worked, because she'd changed. She'd wanted something he'd always believed he hadn't wanted.

On paper, Emmy was just about the worst choice he could make. OK, she was more organised and together than he'd thought she was, but they were still so different. How could it possibly work between them?

Besides, this was meant to be a three-month trial in co-guardianship. Any relationship between them could potentially wreak huge havoc on Tyler's life. She'd said herself that her relationships always failed, and he'd made a mess of his marriage. He just couldn't let himself think of Emmy in any other role than that of co-guardian. No matter how attractive he found her. No matter how much he wanted to kiss those soft, sweet lips until her eyes went all wide and dark with passion.

Not happening, he told himself. Stick to the limits you agreed.

CHAPTER EIGHT

THE FOLLOWING WEEK, Emmy had a phone call that left her shrieking and dancing round the house. She called her mother, and then Dylan.

'Sorry to ring you at work,' she said, 'but I couldn't wait to tell you—the magazine just rang. They loved my designs and they're going to run the feature with me in it. Apparently what swayed them was the seahorse—which was your suggestion, so it's all thanks to you.'

'No worries,' he said, sounding pleased for her. 'But it was just a suggestion. You're the one who did all the hard work.'

'I'm going to stand you a decent meal to say thank you.' She laughed. 'Don't worry, I'm not cooking it myself, so you're in no danger of getting rubbery monkfish again. Mum says she can babysit Ty on Friday or Saturday, whichever suits you best.'

'Emmy, you don't need to take me out.'

'Yes, I do. You more than earned it, taking over all my duties and giving me the time to work, so don't argue. We'll sort out the time when you get home tonight, and I'll book somewhere.' She paused. 'One last thing. They want to take a few shots of me here, at my workbench. Um, this afternoon. Do you have a problem with that?'

'No, it's fine. Do you need me back early to look after Tyler?'

'Hopefully the photographer will be here while Tyler's taking a nap. Or, if he wakes, it won't matter if he's in the shots. If that's OK with you, that is.'

'It's fine,' he said again. 'I'll see you later.'

The journalist arrived while Tyler was still awake, so Emmy made her a coffee and played with the baby while she answered questions, hoping that she didn't come across as too flaky or too distracted. And Tyler decided to forego his nap, so when the photographer arrived—two hours later than they'd arranged—he ended up being in the shots.

They were halfway through the photo shoot when Dylan arrived.

'Sorry—am I in the way?' he asked, coming in to Emmy's workroom.

'No—we're running late,' Emmy said.

Tyler held out his hands to Dylan, who smiled and scooped him into his arms, then kissed him roundly. 'Hello, trouble. Aren't you supposed to be having a nap right now?' he asked.

The baby gurgled and clapped his hands.

'Come on. Let's give Emmy some peace and quiet.' He glanced over at Emmy, the journalist and the photographer. 'I'm about to put the kettle on. Coffee?'

'Thanks, that'd be great,' Emmy said gratefully. 'Oh, sorry, I haven't introduced you. Dylan, this is Mike and Flo from the magazine. Flo, Mike, this is Dylan Harper.'

'Nice to meet you,' Dylan said. 'Milk or sugar?'

'Just milk for me,' Flo said.

'Black, two sugars,' Mike said.

'Back in a tick,' Dylan said, winked at Emmy, and whisked Tyler out of the workroom.

'Wow, he's gorgeous *and* domesticated. The perfect man,' Flo said wistfully.

Just what Emmy was starting to think, though

wild horses wouldn't make her admit it, especially if there was a danger of Dylan overhearing her. 'He has his moments,' she said gruffly.

'You're just so lucky. This house, that cute baby, and that gorgeous man. And you're talented as well. If you weren't so nice, I'd have to hate you,' Flo said.

'Hang on—you've got the wrong end of the stick. Ty's not ours. Well, he *is* ours,' Emmy said, 'but we're not his parents.'

'Adopted? That's lovely.'

'We're his guardians. We were his parents' best friends.' Emmy explained the situation with Ally and Pete as succinctly as she could. 'Dylan and I just share a house and Ty's care.'

Flo raised an eyebrow. 'Just housemates—with the way you two look at each other? Methinks the lady doth protest too much.'

Oh, help. Emmy didn't dare ask Flo to expand on that. Obviously she thought Dylan looked at her as if he were in love with her—which Emmy knew wasn't the case. But she really hoped that she didn't look at him as if she were mooning over him. Because she wasn't. Was she? 'We're just...' Her voice faded.

'Good friends?' Flo asked.

No. They weren't. Though they were on the way to becoming friends. There was a real easiness between them nowadays. 'Something like that,' Emmy said carefully.

'Gotcha.' Flo tapped her nose. 'So what does he do?'

'He's—well, I guess you'd call him a computer superguru,' Emmy said.

Flo scribbled something on her notepad. 'Clever as well as easy on the eye. Nice.'

'Mmm.' Emmy wriggled uncomfortably, and was relieved when the photographer asked her to pose for some more shots and Flo changed the subject back to her work. Something safe. Whereas Dylan Harper was starting to become dangerous.

On Saturday evening, her planned thank-you meal with Dylan felt more like a date. Which was crazy. Though of course she'd had to dress up a bit for it; she couldn't just go out in her usual black trousers and a zany top.

And it felt even more like a date when the taxi arrived and her mother kissed them both goodbye at the door. 'Don't worry, Tyler's in safe hands—just go out and enjoy yourselves. And don't hurry back.'

Emmy felt almost shy with him, and she didn't manage to make any small talk in the taxi. Neither did he, she noticed. Was it because he was a geek with no social skills, or was it because he felt the same kind of awkwardness that she did? The same kind of awareness?

'Nice choice,' Dylan said approvingly when they reached the small Italian restaurant she'd booked. 'And I'm buying champagne. No arguments from you.'

Even though that was pretty much negating the point of the evening, it also broke the ice, and Emmy grinned. 'When have you known me argue with you, Dylan?' she teased.

He laughed back. 'Not for a few weeks, I admit.'

'I really appreciate your support over the article.'

'You would've done the same for me,' he pointed out.

'Well, yes. But it's still appreciated. You put yourself out.'

The waiter ushered them to their table, and the awkwardness returned. Emmy didn't have a clue what to say to Dylan. This was ridiculously like a first date, where you knew hardly anything about each other. She'd lived with him for weeks now and knew a fair bit about what made him tick—what brightened his day, and what he needed before he could be human first thing in the morning—but at the same time he was still virtually a stranger. He hadn't opened up to her about anything emotional. She knew nothing about his childhood or why his marriage broke up or what he really wanted out of life. He kept himself closed off. They were partners of a sort, stand-in parents to their godchild; and yet at the same time they weren't partners at all.

The champagne arrived and Dylan lifted his glass in a toast. 'To you, and every success in that magazine.'

'Thank you.' She lifted her own glass. 'To you, and thanks for—well, being there for me.'

'Any time.'

Given that Dylan didn't have a clue how to be nice to people for the sake of it, she knew he meant it, and it made her feel warm inside.

'It was good of your mum to babysit. She's really nice,' Dylan said.

Was she imagining things, or did he sound wistful? 'Isn't yours?' she asked, before she could stop herself.

'She travels a lot.'

Which told her precisely nothing. She could see that Dylan was busy putting up metaphorical barbed-wire fences with 'keep out' notices stuck to them, so she stuck with the safer topic. 'You're right, my mum's really nice. I'm lucky because she's always been really supportive.' She sighed. 'I just wish I could find someone for her who deserves her.'

Dylan raised an eyebrow. 'Your mum's single?'

She nodded. 'I nag her into dating sometimes. So does her best friend, but she always turns down a second date with whoever it is, or agrees they'd be better off as just friends. I guess she's never found anyone she really trusts.'

He sat and waited, and eventually Emmy found herself telling him the rest of it. 'My father pretty much broke her heart. While they were married, he had a lot of affairs. Now I'm older, I can see that it chipped away at her confidence every time she found out he was seeing some-one.' Just as her own disastrous relationships had chipped away at her confidence, one by one. Every man who'd wanted to change something about her—and it had been a different thing, each time, until in the end the only thing she knew she was good at was her work.

She bit her lip. 'The worst thing is, Mum always wanted more children after me but couldn't have them. He refused to consider adoption or fostering. And then his current woman found out she was pregnant, and he left us for her. Mum felt she'd failed.'

Dylan knew exactly how it felt when your marriage failed and you were pretty sure it was all your fault. First-hand. And it wasn't a good feeling. 'It wasn't your mum's fault,' he said. 'I might be talking out of line, here, but sounds to me as if your dad was incredibly selfish.' Just like his mother. He knew how *that* felt, too, realising that you were way down someone's list of priorities. The amount of times he'd come home from school and let himself into a cold, empty house, and there was a note propped on the kitchen table telling him to go to his grandparents' house because they'd be looking after him for a few days. Days that stretched into weeks.

'My dad was incredibly selfish. He probably still is.'

'Probably?' Dylan was surprised. 'Don't you see him?'

'He didn't stay in touch with us, and for years I thought it was my fault that my parents split up. It was only later, when I'd left university and Mum told me what really went on when I was young, that I realised he was the one with the problem.'

And now Dylan understood why she'd accused him of breaking up his marriage because of an affair. She'd been caught in the fallout from her father's affairs, and it clearly still hurt.

She blew out a breath. 'I think he decided not to see me because whenever he did see me it reminded him of my mum, and that made him start to feel guilty about the way he treated her.'

'So is that why you're single? Because you don't trust men?' And that would certainly explain Spiky Emmy. It was clearly a defence mechanism, and it had definitely worked with him. He'd taken her at face value.

She frowned. 'Not quite. I just have a habit of picking the wrong ones. Men who want to change me—everything from the way I dress, to what I do for a living. Nothing about me is right.'

At one point Dylan would've wanted Emmy to change—but now he knew her better and he understood what made her tick. And he knew that she wasn't the woman he'd thought she was. 'You're fine as you are. There's nothing wrong with what you do for a living. Or how you dress.'

'I wasn't fishing for compliments.' She shrugged. 'I'm tired of dating men who can't see me for who I am or accept me for that. I'm tired of dating men who are all sweetness and light for a couple of weeks, then start making little "helpful" suggestions. All of which mean me changing to fit their expectations, rather than them looking at their expectations and maybe changing them.' She sighed. 'It's not that I think I'm perfect. Of course I'm not. I'm like everyone else, with good points and bad. I just wanted a partner who understands who I am and is OK with that.'

'Maybe,' he said, 'you should've got Ally to vet your dates before you went out with them.'

'I wish I had.' She sighed. 'The last one...' She grimaced and shook her head. 'No, I really don't want to talk about him. But he was definitely my biggest mistake. And he was my last mistake, too. So if you're worrying that I'm going to be flighty and disappear off with the first man who bats his eyelashes at me, leaving you to look after Tyler on your own, then don't. Because I'm not. I've given up looking for Mr Right. I know he isn't out there. My focus now is being there for Tyler while he grows up.'

'So you're not looking for a husband or a family, or what have you?'

'No. But I have Tyler. That's enough for me.'

Before they'd become co-guardians, the Emmy Jacobs Dylan knew was flighty as well as spiky. He'd disliked her because she'd reminded him so much of his mother. Selfish, always apologising for being late but never seeming sincere.

Now, he was seeing a different side of her. The way she looked after Tyler and put the baby's needs first: she was definitely responsible. She was kind; without being intrusive, she'd worked out what he liked to eat and the fact that he loathed lentils, and changed her meal plans to suit. She was thoughtful. And she was fiercely independent; from what she'd just told him about her childhood, he could understand exactly why she wouldn't want to rely on someone. She'd seen her mother's heart broken and had learned from that.

And he didn't want Spiky Emmy back. He liked the woman he'd got to know. More than liked her, if he was honest with himself. 'I'm not worried at all,' he said lightly. 'You didn't need to tell me that. I already know you're not flighty.'

'Oh.' She looked slightly deflated, as if she'd been gearing up to have a fight with him and now she didn't have to. 'So what about you? Are you looking for Ms Right?'

'No, I made enough of a mess of my marriage.' And then he surprised himself by adding, 'And it was my fault.'

'How? You didn't have an affair.'

'Neither did Nadine.'

'So what went wrong?' She put a hand to her mouth. 'Sorry. I know I shouldn't ask you personal stuff.'

Absolutely. He didn't want to talk about his feelings or his past. But he surprised himself even more by saying, 'Given our situation, you probably ought to know. And I know you're not going to gossip about me.'

'Of course I'm not.'

'Nadine and I—we wanted the same things, at first. A satisfying career, knowing we could reach the top of our respective trees. Neither of us wanted kids. Except then she changed her mind.'

'And you didn't?'

He shook his head. 'She gave me an ultimatum: baby or divorce. So I picked the latter.'

She blew out a breath. 'And now you're in exactly that situation with Tyler—a stand-in dad. Though obviously you and I—we're not...'

Her voice faded, and he wondered if she was thinking about that kiss. He most definitely was. He forced himself to focus. 'Yeah.' But his voice sounded slightly rusty to his ears. He hoped she wouldn't guess why.

'So does that mean...I mean, the three months are up in a couple of weeks. And you don't want to...?' She looked worried.

'I'm glad you brought that up,' he said. 'It's working for me. I think we're a good team. I know we're never going to be as good as Pete and Ally, and I for one still have a lot to learn about babies, but Tyler seems happy with us.'

'Are *you* happy?' she asked.

'Yes. And I feel a bit guilty about it. I said I didn't want to be a parent. But, actually, I'm enjoying it,' he confessed. It was a relief to admit it out loud, at last. 'I like coming home to a baby. I like seeing him change. I like hearing him babble and I like seeing his face when he tries something new.'

'Me, too,' she said softly.

'So we keep going?' he asked.

'What about your ex?'

He grimaced. 'As I said, I feel guilty. Maybe it could've worked, if I hadn't been so stubborn. Or maybe it wouldn't. I don't know.'

'Why didn't you want a child?' she asked.

He blew out a breath. 'I just don't. Didn't.'

'You mean, back off because you don't want to talk about it?' she asked wryly.

He was slightly surprised that she'd read him so well. 'Yes. Tonight's meant to be about toast-

ing your success, not dragging through my fail-
ures. So, yes, I'd rather change the subject. I'm
not the kind of guy who talks about my feelings
and wallows in things,' Dylan said. 'I just get
things done. With the social skills of a rhino.'

She gave him a rueful smile. 'You're never
going to let me forget that, are you?'

'No. Because, actually, it's true,' he said. 'Anyway. The main thing is that we both know where
we stand—we're both single, and we're both
planning to stay that way. And we can just get
on with looking after Tyler.'

'Yeah.' She raised her glass again. 'To Tyler. I
wish things could've been different—but I think
we're managing to be the next best option for
him. Even if we do have to rely on looking things
up in a book or asking my mum, half the time.'

'Absolutely.' He clinked his glass against hers.
'To Tyler, and to being the best stand-in parents
he could ever have.'

Somehow the awkwardness between them had
vanished, and Emmy was surprised at how easy
it was to talk to Dylan. And to discover that

they had shared loves in music and places they wanted to visit.

She was beginning to see why Pete and Ally had made that decision, now. She and Dylan had their differences, which would be good for Tyler; but they also had much more overlap than either of them had ever imagined. She actually liked his company.

And she was shocked by how late it was when she finally glanced at her watch. 'We'd better call a taxi. And I'd better ring Mum and let her know we're on our way back.'

'You ring your mum, and I'll call the cab,' Dylan said.

In the taxi, their hands kept brushing against each other, and it felt as if little electric shocks were running through her veins. Which was crazy. Dylan was the last man she could afford to be attracted to. This shouldn't be happening.

But what if it did?

What if Dylan held her hand?

And then she stopped breathing for a second when his fingers curled round hers. Was he thinking the same as she was?

She met his gaze, and the remaining breath whooshed out of her lungs.

Yes. He was.

She wasn't sure which of them moved first, but then his hand was cupping her cheek, hers was curled into his hair, and his mouth was brushing against hers. Slow, soft, gentle kisses. Exploring. Enticing. Promising.

He drew her closer and the kiss deepened. Hot enough to make her toes curl and her skin feel too tight. This was what she wanted. What they both wanted.

And then she was horribly aware of a light going on and someone coughing.

The taxi driver.

Clearly they were home. And they'd been caught in a really embarrassing position.

She looked at Dylan, aghast. Oh, no. This was a bad move. Yes, she wanted him and he wanted her. But what would happen when it all went wrong? Tyler would be the one who paid the price.

So they were going to have to be sensible about this. Stop it before it started.

'Um. That shouldn't have happened,' she muttered, unable to look him in the eye.

'Absolutely,' he agreed, to her mingled relief and regret. 'Blame it on the champagne. And it won't happen again,' he added.

Which ought to make her feel relieved. Instead, it made her feel miserable.

'Go in. I'll pay the driver.'

'Thanks.' She fled before she said or did anything else stupid. And tonight, she thought, tonight she'd have a cold shower and hope that her common sense came back—and stayed there.

CHAPTER NINE

DYLAN PUT THE phone down and leaned back against his chair, his eyes closed.

This was potentially a huge deal.

And it came with an equally huge sticking point: the client was a family man who liked to work with people who had the same outlook on life.

Strictly speaking, Dylan wasn't a family man. He was an almost-divorcee who happened to have co-guardianship of his godson. His marriage breakdown would certainly count against him; and his arrangement with Emmy was hardly conventional.

Could he ask her to help him out?

After all, he'd helped her when she'd needed it. And she *had* offered...

He thought about buying her flowers, but that would be manipulative and tacky. No, he'd just ask her once Tyler was in bed. Talk it over with her. And maybe she'd have a creative way round the situation—because Emmy definitely had a different take on life from his.

It helped a bit that it was his turn to cook that night. And he totally appreciated now why she'd tried to cook the monkfish. Except he played it safe, with pasta. 'Emmy, can I ask you a favour?' he asked over dinner.

'Sure. What?'

'I've put in a tender for a project.'

She looked thoughtful. 'So you're going to be working longer hours and need me to pick up the slack for a bit? That's fine, because you did exactly that for me. Of course I'll do it.'

He grimaced. 'Not exactly. I'm learning to delegate, so I don't need you to pick up the slack. Anyway, I haven't got the deal yet.'

She frowned. 'So if you don't need me to take over from you, what's the favour, then?'

This was the biggie. 'The client. He's a family man. He likes to work with—well, people who have the same outlook.'

She raised an eyebrow. 'Isn't that discrimination?'

'It would be, if he was employing me,' Dylan agreed, 'but this is different. It's a project and my company's put in a bid for it, so the client can choose his contractor however he likes.'

'And you want him to think you're a family man?' She looked wary. 'Dylan, this is a seriously bad idea. You're not a family man.'

'I'm Tyler's co-guardian, so *technically* that makes me a family man.'

'But you and I...' Her voice faded and she looked slightly shocked. 'Oh, no. Please tell me you're not expecting me to lie for you and pretend that you and I are an item?'

'I'm not expecting you to lie. Just...' How could he put this nicely? 'Just fudge the issue a little.'

She shook her head. 'It'll backfire. When he realises you lied—and he *will* realise, if you get the contract and he works with you—then he'll have no faith in you. Professionally as well as personally. Which will be a disaster for your business.'

He folded his arms. 'What happened to looking out for each other?'

She narrowed her eyes at him. 'I *am* looking out for you, Dylan. This isn't the best way forward, and you know I'm right.'

There wasn't much he could say to that, so he remained silent.

'But,' she said, 'I'll help you. Invite him round to dinner. I'll cook.'

He looked at her. 'Thank you for the offer, but I think I'll pass on that one.'

She rolled her eyes. 'You're not going to let me forget that monkfish, are you?'

'It was pretty bad,' he said. 'Not that I could do any better myself. Which is why I think inviting him to dinner's a bad idea. The kitchen isn't my forte or yours.' He frowned. 'Though I suppose I could buy something from the supermarket that I just have to put in the oven and heat through.' His frown deepened. 'But could I ask you to do the table setting, please?'

She gave him a sidelong look. 'Because I'm a girl?'

'No. Because you have an artist's eye and you're good at that sort of thing,' he corrected.

* * *

He'd actually paid her a compliment. A genuine one. And Emmy was surprised by how warm it made her feel.

'Of course I'll do the table setting. But this meal needs to be home-cooked if you invite him round. We can't just give him a ready meal from the supermarket.' She thought for a moment. 'OK. If he's a family man, invite his wife and kids. We'll make it a family meal.'

His eyes narrowed. 'So what are you planning? Are you going to talk your mum into cooking for us?'

She shook her head. 'I don't need to. We'll keep it simple. Something like…hmm. A roast dinner.'

He grimaced. 'I remember the student house I shared with Pete. The four of us made our first Christmas dinner and the turkey wasn't properly cooked. We were all ill for three days afterwards.'

'This isn't a student house. And I'll ask my mum about timings so it won't go wrong. How old are his kids?'

'I have no idea.'

'Find out.' She looked thoughtful. 'Actually, if they're little, they won't have the patience for a starter, and if they're teens they probably won't want to come anyway. So we'll skip the starter. We can do a roast dinner for the main, and fresh fruit salad and ice cream for dessert. We're both working and we're looking after Tyler, so it's OK to take the odd short cut.'

'But you'll be there at the table, won't you? You're not just going to be in the kitchen?'

'Why, Dylan, anyone would think you wanted me there,' she teased.

He gave her a speaking look. 'All right. You can have your pound of flesh. I want you there. You have good social skills.'

'Thank you.' She grinned and punched his arm. 'And yours are a bit better than they were. Go and ring him. Find out if there's anything they can't eat—either because of allergies or because they hate it. And we definitely need to know if anyone's vegetarian.'

'Because then we'll have to rethink the menu?'

'Because then dinner will be pasta,' she said.

'We can both cook that. And we'll serve it with garlic bread and salad. Simple and homely.'

Dylan rang his potential client the next morning, and then rang Emmy. 'It'll be just Ted Burroughs and his wife. You were right about the kids—they're teens, and he says they'll pass on the invite.' He smiled. 'Mind you, he has girls. If I'd said I live with a top jewellery designer...'

'No, they would've been bored with the conversation, so it's better that they don't come,' Emmy said. 'What about the food?'

'No allergies, and he appreciated you asking.' He paused. 'I appreciate you, too. I wouldn't have thought of that.'

'Which is because,' she said, 'you only have one X chromosome.'

'That's *so* sexist.'

She laughed. 'Bite me, Dylan.'

She was adorable in this playful mood.

Then Dylan caught his thoughts and was shocked at the fact he'd used the word 'adorable' about her. What was happening? Emmy Jacobs was his co-guardian, and that was all.

The kisses and the hand-holding in the taxi had been…well, mistakes.

Even if he did want to repeat them.

Even if a little, secret part of him thought that yes, he'd like to be partners with Emmy in more than just sharing Tyler's care.

'See you later,' he said. 'And thanks.'

The day of the dinner arrived, and Dylan made sure that he was home early to help. Emmy had already set the dining room table with candles, fresh flowers, a damask tablecloth and silver-ware, and the chicken was in the oven.

'Is there anything you need me to do?' he asked.

'Make a start on peeling the potatoes?' she suggested.

He did so, and noticed that there was a list held onto the fridge with a magnet. 'What's this?'

'The timing plan for dinner,' she said. 'And I'm using the oven timer to make sure I don't miss anything.'

She definitely looked strained, he thought. 'Stop worrying. I'm sure it will be fine.'

'That's not what you said when I first suggested cooking a roast dinner.'

He rolled his eyes. 'OK, O Wise One. You were right and you know better than I do.'

'I hope so.' Though she didn't sound convinced.

'So you got the timings from a book?' he asked.

'Better than that—Mum helped. She did offer to come and cook for us, but I thought that'd be cheating.'

Would it? he wondered.

She'd obviously caught the expression on his face just before he masked it, because she sighed. 'You think I should've taken her up on the offer, don't you?'

'No, I'm sure all will be just fine.' He finished peeling the potatoes. 'Do you want me to make the fruit salad?'

'It's already done so the flavours can mingle.' Almost on cue, there was the sound of gurgling and cooing from the baby listener. She smiled. 'It sounds like someone's just woken. Go and play with Tyler—you're getting under my feet and being annoying.' She shooed him out of the kitchen, though he was careful to make sure that she really didn't need any help before he agreed to go.

He spent some time playing with the baby. Again it surprised him just how much he was en-joying this domestic set-up. He'd never thought a family was for him; or maybe Nadine just hadn't been the right person for him to have a family with. He pushed away the thought that maybe Emmy was the right one. He knew she had is-sues about relationships, and he wasn't sure how it could work between them. They couldn't risk fracturing Tyler's world again.

Emmy ticked off everything she'd done on her list, checked the list a second time in case she'd missed anything, and then did a final read-through just to be absolutely certain.

Everything was ready, as far as it could be. Barring having to rescue everything from a last-minute catastrophe in the kitchen—and she hoped she'd done enough planning to avoid that—there was nothing else to do.

She changed into a simple black dress and some of her more delicate jewellery, and adopted the 'less is more' principle when it came to her make-up. She stared at herself critically in the mirror. How many of her ex-boyfriends hadn't been happy with the way she looked? The colour of her hair, the fact that it rarely stayed the same colour for more than a couple of months at a time, the way she dressed...

She took a deep breath. Dylan wasn't her boyfriend, and she looked just fine. Professional. Competent.

All the same, when she came back down into the kitchen, she grabbed an apron, just in case she spilled anything over herself while she was cooking.

Dylan was already there, feeding Tyler in his high chair. The baby beamed and banged his hands on his tray when he saw her.

'Hello, Gorgeous. Is Uncle Dylan in charge of dinner tonight?'

'Dih-dih.' Tyler gurgled with pleasure—and bits of carrot sprayed all over Dylan's shirt.

'Oops. Sorry,' she said.

He flapped a dismissive hand, then grinned.

'What?' she asked suspiciously.

'If anyone had ever told me I'd see you wearing an apron, looking all domestic...'

'Oh, ha ha.' She rolled her eyes. 'Ty, make sure you spit more carrot at him.'

Dylan just laughed. 'We're about done here. I'll sort out bath and bed. Is there anything else you need?'

'No—I'm fine. And you'd better change, Dylan—you've got mashed carrot on your shirt.'

'I guess so.'

It wasn't that long ago that Dylan had been so formal and stuffy that even his jeans were ironed and his T-shirts were pristine and white. He'd unbent an awful lot if he wasn't that fussed about mashed carrot on one of his work shirts, Emmy thought, especially as she knew carrot could stain.

She fussed around downstairs while Dylan sorted out Tyler's bath and bedtime, and changed his shirt. And then the doorbell went, and her stomach went into knots. This deal could mean as much for Dylan's business as the magazine thing meant for hers so she really couldn't afford to mess things up tonight. If the veg wasn't cooked enough or, worse, cooked to a mush...

Breathe, she told herself. Everything's going to be just fine. You've used the timer and ticked everything off the list. It's not going to let you down and you're not going to let Dylan down.

Dylan answered the door; she stayed in the kitchen for just a little longer, nerving herself, then came out to meet their guests.

'Emmy, this is Ted and Elaine Burroughs— Ted and Elaine, this is Emmy Jacobs,' Dylan introduced them.

'Delighted to meet you. Thank you for having us,' Ted said, and shook her hand warmly.

Emmy was horribly aware that she was still wearing her apron. So much for being sophisticated. 'Um, sorry, I hope you'll excuse...' She indicated the apron with an embarrassed grimace.

'Of course,' Ted said.

'So how long have you been together?' Elaine asked.

Emmy and Dylan exchanged a glance.

Be honest, she willed him. Tell them the truth, or it'll come back to bite you.

'We're not actually a couple, as such,' Dylan said. 'We share a house. And we're also co-guardians of Tyler, our best friends' son—they were killed in a car crash three months ago. They'd asked us both to look after Tyler if anything happened to them. So here we are.'

'So you moved out of your own homes and in here together?' Elaine asked.

'It was the best thing for Tyler,' Emmy said. 'He needed to be somewhere familiar.'

'Plus my flat in Docklands wasn't really baby-friendly,' Dylan added.

'And mine in Camden was only big enough for me, not for the three of us,' Emmy explained.

'That must have been hard for you,' Ted said, his face full of sympathy.

'We've been thrown in a bit at the deep end,' Emmy said, 'but we're managing. I should tell you now that dinner's not totally a home-made thing. I'm afraid we cheated and bought the gravy and the ice cream, but I hope you'll forgive us for that.'

'My dear, it's very kind of you to invite us over—especially given your circumstances,' Elaine said.

'We support each other,' Emmy said. 'Sometimes Dylan has a late meeting and needs me to pick up the slack, and sometimes I have a rush on at work and need him to hold the fort for me.' She exchanged a glance with him. 'And he's better than I am at getting Ty to sleep. He sings better.'

'That always worked with our two,' Elaine said with a smile.

'Would you excuse me?' Emmy asked. 'I need to check on the veg. Dylan, can you—'

'—sort the drinks?' he finished. 'Sure. Would you like to come through to the dining room, Elaine and Ted?'

He sorted out the drinks while she did the last-minute things in the kitchen. She was putting the vegetables in serving dishes when she overheard Elaine complimenting the table setting.

'That's all down to Emmy,' Dylan said. 'She has an artist's eye. You should see her jewellery—it's amazing, so delicate and pretty.'

It warmed her to know he was being absolutely serious. Dylan never gushed.

She brought the serving dishes and warmed plates through, and Dylan carved the chicken.

To her relief, the food seemed to go down well. The vegetables were fine—not too hard or too soft—and she'd managed to get the potatoes crispy on the outside and fluffy inside, thanks to her mother's instructions.

'Dylan tells us you're a jeweller,' Elaine said. 'Our eldest daughter is about to turn sixteen, and I know she'd like some jewellery for her birthday. Could you make some for her?'

'Sure,' Emmy said. 'Most of the stuff on my website is either in stock or won't take long to make, or I could design something especially for her.'

'Why don't you show Elaine the pieces you made for the magazine?' Dylan suggested. 'Or is that embargoed?'

'Officially it's embargoed,' Emmy confirmed, 'but I guess it's OK for you to see the photographs I took. Excuse me a second?' She grabbed her phone from her bag, and showed Elaine the photographs.

'That really delicate stuff—that's so Claire. She'd love something like that,' Elaine said.

'Do you want it to be a surprise? If not, you could bring Claire over and I can talk to her about what she'd really like, and design it for her there and then.' Emmy smiled. 'Actually, why don't you do that and we can make it a really girly session? It'll make her feel special to have something designed just for her.' She put a hand on Dylan's arm. 'Sorry, this wasn't meant to be about my business tonight. I didn't mean to take over.'

He smiled. 'You weren't taking over. I just think what you make is really amazing. She does these jet carvings as well, little animals. She made me a fantastic bear.'

'Teddy?' Ted asked with a grin.

Dylan laughed back. 'Ah, no. It's a grizzly. She was making a point,' Dylan said.

'You're lucky I didn't make you a rhino,' she teased.

'A rhino?' Elaine looked mystified.

'Because she says I have the same level of social skills as a rhino,' Dylan explained. 'I guess it goes with being good at maths.'

'You're a total geek,' she said, but her tone was affectionate.

She cleared the table and brought out the fruit

salad; she'd bought thin heart-shaped shortbread from the deli and vanilla ice cream to go with it.

'Pineapple, raspberries, kiwi and pomegranate,' Elaine said as she looked at the bowl. 'How lovely. I'd never thought of making a fruit salad like that. You really are good in the kitchen.'

'Not always,' Emmy confessed. 'I tried making monkfish in parma ham a few weeks back, and it was absolutely terrible. That's why we decided to cook a roast dinner tonight, because it's much simpler and less likely to go wrong. And I still had to call my mum for the timings and instructions on the roast potatoes.'

'You did her proud, love,' Ted said.

Emmy found herself relaxing now that the trickiest part of the meal was over. But then Tyler woke, and they could all hear him crying on the baby listener.

'I'll go,' Emmy said.

'No, it's my shift,' Dylan said.

'Not anymore,' she corrected him. 'I put a sticky note on the board so it's my shift. You stay with our guests.' She realised her slip almost immediately, but hoped she hadn't messed

it up. It had felt so natural to call the Burroughses 'our' guests rather than 'your'.

'I'd love to see the baby,' Elaine said wistfully.
'But I guess you can't bring him down as it'll
put him out of his routine.'

'You can come up to the nursery with me, if
you like,' she offered impulsively, and Elaine
beamed.

'I'd love to.'

And maybe this would give Dylan and Ted
the chance to discuss business, Emmy thought.

Elaine clearly loved having the chance to cuddle a baby. 'How old is he?'

'Seven months, now.'

'You forget how cute they are at this age. He'll
be crawling, next.'

'And we'll have baby gates all over the place,'
Emmy said with a smile.

She settled the baby down in his cot again, and
put his light show on.

'It's very sad about your friends,' Elaine said,
'and it must be difficult for you. How are you
both coping?'

'It was pretty tough at first,' Emmy admitted.
'Dylan wasn't a very hands-on godfather when

Tyler was really tiny. I guess he was waiting to do all the stuff like kicking a ball round in the park, going to the boating lake, and helping teach him to ride a bike—stuff I wouldn't do as a godmother, because I'd rather take him swimming or to baby music classes. But we've muddled through together for the last three months, and it helps that we take alternate night shifts.' She blew out a breath. 'It means we each manage to get one good night's sleep out of two. I have no idea how my best friend coped the way she did. She always looked fresh as a daisy, even if the baby had been up half a dozen times in the night.'

'You must miss her,' Elaine said.

'I do—and Dylan really misses Pete. They were the nearest we had to a brother and sister.'

'But Dylan helps you now.'

Emmy nodded. 'He's been brilliant. Actually, he's helped right from the start, even though he's never had anything to do with babies before and was obviously scared to death that he'd do something wrong and hurt the baby. He's never just left me to deal with everything; he's always done his fair share, even if it involves dirty nappies or having stuff dribbled all over him. He's stubborn and sometimes he comes across as a bit closed off or he says totally the wrong thing, but his heart's in the right place and he thinks things through properly.' She smiled. 'Don't tell him I said this, but when we do argue he's usually right.'

Elaine smiled back. 'He sounds like my Ted.'

Emmy checked the cot once more; satisfied that Tyler had settled again, she ushered Elaine back downstairs to the dining room. She made coffee and brought in the posh chocolate truffles she'd found in the deli, and helped Dylan make small talk until the Burroughses finally left.

Dylan helped her clear up. 'By the way, do you know the baby listener was still on when you were upstairs with Elaine?'

Emmy looked at him, horrified. 'You're kidding!'

He shook his head.

'How much did you hear?' she demanded.

'Let me think.' He spread his hands. 'That would be…' He met her gaze. 'All of it.'

She closed her eyes briefly. Obviously she'd wrecked everything, because she just hadn't been able to keep her mouth shut. 'I'm so sorry, Dylan. Ted must've thought...' She bit her lip.

'He was laughing.' Dylan's eyes crinkled at the corners. 'Especially at the bit when you said I'm usually right. And I hope you realise I have every intention of using that one against you in the future.'

She knew that was an attempt to stop her worrying, and ignored it. 'I just hope I haven't screwed up the deal for you.'

'I think,' he said, 'you showed Ted what he wanted to know. That I'm not just this efficient machine.'

'Well, you're that as well.'

Dylan raised an eyebrow. 'Thank you. If that was meant to be a compliment.'

'A backhanded one,' she confirmed.

He smiled at her. 'That's what I like about you. You never sugar-coat stuff.'

'There's no point. I've had it with charm.'

'Ouch.' He looked serious. 'Want to talk about it?'

'We already have. I told you I had rubbish taste in men. That's just another example. I fall for the charm every time—hook, line and sinker.'

He reached over and stroked her cheek, and every nerve-end in her skin zinged. 'Something I should tell you. You're usually right, too, when we argue. You make me think things through in a different way. And that's a good thing.'

'Think outside the regular tetrahedron?' she asked

'There's absolutely nothing regular tetrahedron about you, Emmy.'

'Thank you. If that was meant to be a compliment,' she threw back at him.

His eyes crinkled at the corners again. And how ridiculous that it made her heart skip a beat.

'It was. And thank you for your help. You might just have made the difference.' He looked at her mouth. 'Emmy. You were brilliant, tonight.' His voice deepened, grew huskier. And then he leaned forward and pressed the lightest, sweetest kiss against her lips.

It was anatomically impossible, but he made her feel as if her heart had just turned over. How could she help herself resting her palm against his cheek, feeling the faint prickle of stubble against her fingertips? Especially when his hands slid down her sides, resting lightly against her hips as he drew her closer.

Then she panicked. She couldn't feel like this about Dylan. She just couldn't. She took a step back. 'We…'

'Yeah. I know. Sorry.' He raked a hand through his hair. 'That didn't happen.'

'No. It was just adrenaline, because we were both panicking about dinner.'

'Absolutely,' he said as she took another step back. 'I'll finish up in here. You go and…' He blew out a breath. 'Whatever. I'll see you later.'

She took the hint and made herself scarce. Before she did something really stupid, like kissing him again.

CHAPTER TEN

DYLAN WAS TWITCHY for the next couple of days, though Emmy understood why. She'd been in the same situation herself, not so long ago.

On Saturday morning at breakfast, she said, 'Right, you need to get out of the house.'

'What?' Dylan looked at her as if she were speaking Martian.

'Waiting. It's the pits. And if you stay in and try and concentrate on work, you'll end up brooding. So you're coming out with Ty and me to get some fresh air. Isn't he, Ty?'

The baby gurgled and banged his spoon against the tray of his high chair. 'Dih-dih!'

'It sounds as if you have something in mind,' Dylan said.

Emmy nodded. 'I've been making a list of places to go with him. We can always go to the park with the slide and the swings on sunny days, but it's no good on rainy or cold days. And this is one I've been looking forward to.'

She was mysterious about where they were going, and Dylan didn't have a clue until they were standing outside what looked like an Edwardian greenhouse with a large banner that proclaimed it to be the House of Butterflies.

When they were inside, he discovered that the greenhouse was full of lush vegetation and had a slightly humid, warm atmosphere. He could hear the sound of water falling, so he realised there must be a fountain somewhere. There were butterflies of all sizes and colours, some huge and vivid. He'd never seen so many in one place before.

Ty seemed to love it, watching the butterflies opening and closing their wings as they perched on a flower or fluttered overhead. He reached out to them, waggling his fingers as if copying the movement of their wings.

'Look—those people over there are standing very still, and the butterflies are landing on them,' Emmy exclaimed, looking enchanted.

She tried it herself, and her face was suffused

with wonder when a butterfly landed on her. Dylan wished for a second that he had a camera to capture that expression.

They wandered through the different sections of the enormous greenhouse, looking at the butterflies and the flowers; Dylan was surprised by how much it made him relax.

'Thank you for bringing me here. I was getting a bit scratchy. Sorry, I haven't been very nice to live with.'

She patted his arm, and the feel of her skin against his made him tingle. 'That's OK. I was the same when I was waiting. And you did the same for me, when you took me to the sea,' she said. 'I just thought this might be something different.'

'I would never have thought to go to a butterfly house.'

'To be fair, it hasn't been open for that long, so you probably wouldn't have known about it.' She smiled at him. 'Do you mind if I take a few photos?'

'Sure, go ahead. I'll take Ty.'

He took over the pushchair, and she took various photographs with her phone. Including, to his surprise, the roof of the greenhouse. He'd expected her to concentrate on the butterflies. Then again, Emmy seemed to see things in a different way from most people.

In the next section, there was a terrarium full of chrysalises, and they could actually see some of the pupae emerging from their cocoons.

'That's amazing. I never saw anything like that when I was a kid,' Dylan said.

'Did you have a garden?'

He nodded. 'My grandparents had a huge garden, and my gran loved butterflies and bees—she had shrubs to attract them. My grandfather preferred the more practical stuff, growing fruit and vegetables. And I used to have to help weed the garden whenever I was there.'

'Sounds as if you weren't keen.'

'I was a child,' he said. 'But I've never had a garden since.'

And they'd neglected Pete and Ally's garden, just mowing the lawn.

In the section after, there was a waterfall and a pond with huge red and white goldfish. Emmy unbuckled Tyler from his pushchair and held him up so he had a good view of the pond. 'See the red fish, Ty?'

'Fiiih,' said the little boy.

He saw the shock on Emmy's face and the way she suddenly held Tyler that little bit tighter, as if she'd been near to dropping him. 'Did you hear that, Dylan? He said "fish"!'

'I heard.' And it was crazy to feel so proud of him. Then again, Tyler was the nearest he'd ever get to having a son. Something he'd always thought he didn't want, but now he knew he did.

Tyler clapped his hands with delight, and Emmy beamed at him. 'Clever boy.'

This, Emmy thought, was the perfect day. Tyler learning a new word. Sharing this amazing spectacle with him and with Dylan. And the butterfly house definitely seemed to have taken Dylan's mind off the wait to hear from Ted Burroughs.

In the next section, Dylan found a giant stripy caterpillar and pointed it out to the baby. 'Hey, Tyler, what pillar doesn't need holding up? A caterpillar!'

He chuckled, and the baby laughed back. And Emmy was enchanted. The joke was terrible, but

Stuffy Dylan would never have done something like that. He was definitely changing and she really liked the man he was becoming.

'We'll have to take him to the zoo. I've noticed he really likes that tiger story you bought him,' she said.

'Maybe we could go next weekend?' he suggested. 'Though it's your weekend off.'

'No, that'd be good. I'd like that.'

'And maybe we can look at planting things in the garden,' he said, 'flowers that butterflies really like. Then, next summer, when Tyler plays in the garden he might get to see a few butterflies.'

And maybe it would also bring back nice memories of his grandmother, Emmy thought. Dylan had mentioned her before; and she had the strongest feeling that he'd been closer to his grandmother than he was to his mother. He certainly missed her, from what he'd let slip.

'That's a great idea,' she said. 'Though I had a flat so I'm afraid I'm not much of a gardener. I tended to have cut flowers rather than house-plants. Ally bought me a couple and…well, let's just say I don't have green fingers.'

'We'll learn,' he said. 'Looking after a garden can't be any harder than bringing up a baby, and we're managing fine with Tyler.'

Emmy felt warm inside that not only were they working together as a team, he was also acknowledging that. And this was beginning to feel like being part of a real family. It was taking time, but they were finally bonding.

She was fascinated by the terrarium with the dragonflies in the next section. 'Just look at the colours,' she said, pointing them out to Tyler. 'Blue and green dragonflies.'

'Fiiih,' the baby said again.

She laughed and rubbed the tip of her nose against his. 'Fly, sweetie, not fish. But I guess they both sort of have scales.'

When they stopped in the café, she mashed a banana for Tyler and leaned down to feed him in his pushchair while Dylan went to get the coffee. When Tyler had finished, she scooped him onto her lap and cuddled him with one arm while she made a couple of quick sketches in the notebook she always carried in her handbag.

Dylan put the coffees on the table, out of Tyler's reach. 'What are you doing?' he asked.

'Just noting down a couple of ideas for jewellery.'

He looked intrigued. 'So this sort of thing is where you get your inspiration?'

'Sort of,' she hedged.

'Sorry, is this a creative thing? You don't like to talk about work in progress?'

'No, it's fine.' She felt relaxed enough with him to know that he wasn't like her exes—he was asking because he was interested, not because he wanted her to stop or thought he had better ideas that she ought to go along with. She pushed her notebook across the table to him. 'Have a look through if you want to. Sometimes I take pictures, sometimes I sketch.'

He flicked through the pages. 'That spiderweb reminds me a bit of that necklace you made.'

'With the heart in the middle rather than the spider?' She smiled. 'You're right, that was the inspiration. It was a frosty morning and the cobwebs were really visible. They looked incredibly pretty, delicate yet strong at the same time.'

He reached the page where she'd sketched a couple of pictures of Tyler asleep. 'I had no idea you could draw. I mean, I knew you designed stuff, but that's not the same as a portrait. These are really good.'

'Thank you. I was working while he was napping and I just thought he looked so cute and peaceful. I couldn't resist it.'

He handed the book back to her. 'Very cute. So you carry a notebook all the time?'

'Yes. Because you never know when you're going to see something that sets off an idea,' she explained. 'Though I guess it's not quite like that with your job.'

He smiled. 'No, it's talking to the client that does that.' He indicated the slice of chocolate cake he'd bought. 'Would you like some of this?'

'Thanks, but I'm fine.' Mr Stuffy had changed absolutely, Emmy thought. A couple of months ago, he would barely have spoken to her. Now he was offering to share cake with her, for all the world as if they were partners.

Though she knew better than to kid herself. Yes, Dylan was attractive. Especially when you saw past the superficial eye-candy stuff to the real smile, the one that lit up his eyes. He could tempt her to break every single one of her rules and fall in love with him.

But then what? She couldn't take the risk. If she had an affair with Dylan, she knew it would be amazing at first. But then it would go the way of all her other relationships and end in tears. Hers.

Dylan flicked through the leaflet he'd picked up at the counter. 'Did you know that a butterfly tastes through its feet?'

She raised an eyebrow. 'You expect me to believe that?'

'Seriously, a butterfly can't bite or chew food. It just sucks everything up with a proboscis, so it has to taste things through sensors in its feet.'

'Did you hear that, Ty?' She traced circles on his palm, making the baby giggle.

'Round and round the garden,' Dylan said.

He knew this? Then again, she'd noticed what he'd been reading. He'd left child development books in the living room. Being Dylan, he took things seriously and did it the geek way. 'Like a teddy bear,' she said.

'One step.' He put a finger on Tyler's wrist.

'Two step.' She put a finger on Tyler's elbow.

'And a tickle under there.' He tickled Tyler

under the armpit, and the baby's rich chuckle rang out.

'Come to me so Em can drink her coffee?' Dylan asked, holding his arms out.

Tyler echoed him, holding his arms out to be picked up. 'Dih-dih!'

Dylan scooped him up. 'How did he do with the banana?'

'He ate about three-quarters of it.'

'Good boy. Is the milk in his bag?'

'Sure is.' And how Dylan had come on as a father, she thought. In the early days, he'd been wary, unsure of himself. Now, he was confident, and Tyler responded to that. The baby clearly adored him.

She could easily adore Dylan, too—the man he'd become.

But she needed to keep her burgeoning feelings under control. This was as good as it was going to get, so she was going to enjoy it for what it was and not let herself wish for more. Even though, secretly, she did wish for more.

They really did look cute together, Tyler cuddled on Dylan's lap, holding his own bottle and yet with Dylan's hand held just under it as a safety net. She couldn't resist taking a picture on her phone. 'That's lovely. I'll send it to Ally's and Pete's parents.'

'I was talking to them the other night,' Dylan said. 'They told me you write to them every week with pictures and updates.'

She shrugged. 'Well, they don't really use email. It's nearly the same, just that I print it out rather than send it electronically. It's not a big deal.'

'It's nice of you to bother, though.'

'Just because they've lost their children, it doesn't mean they have to lose their grandson as well,' she said. Then an idea hit her. 'Would you like to send a copy of this photo to your mum? I could send it to your phone, or even directly to her if that's easier for you.'

'No, it's OK.' But it was as if she'd thrown up a brick wall between them, because he went quiet on her.

What had she said?

They'd talked about sending a picture to Tyler's grandparents and she'd suggested sending it to his own mother, too. And it wasn't the first time he'd gone quiet on her after the subject of his parents had cropped up.

Clearly there was some kind of rift there, and she'd just trampled on a really sore spot.

'I'm sorry, Dylan. I didn't mean to...' Help. Given that the intensely private man seemed to be back, how could she phrase this without making it worse? 'I'm sorry,' she said again.

He sighed. 'It's not your fault. Sorry. I'm stressing about the contract. I shouldn't take it out on you.'

She let it go, but still she wondered. She'd noticed that Dylan's mother had never visited or even called the house. He'd said before that his mother was travelling, so maybe she was somewhere with poor phone connections, or maybe she just called him during office hours, when he wasn't in the house. But it was as if almost everything to do with Dylan's family was in a box marked 'extra private, do not touch'.

They still hadn't quite got that easiness and family feeling back by the time they'd finished in the café and went to the gift shop.

Until she spied the butterfly mobile. 'That's lovely. We can put it over his cot. It'd look great with the stars from his nightlight floating over it, and he'll see it first thing in the morning when he wakes.'

'Mmm.' Dylan didn't sound that enthusiastic, but she knew he secretly liked the nightlight.

They continued to browse, and Dylan picked up a board book. 'We need to get this.'

She glanced at it; it was a story about a caterpillar, and there was a finger puppet. So New Dylan was back. Stuffy Dylan might have read a grudging bedtime story, but New Dylan would read it with voices and props so a child would really enjoy it. She grinned. 'You like doing bedtime stories, don't you?'

'Yes. If anyone had told me I'd like doing all the voices, I would've said they were crazy. But I do.' He looked a bit wistful. 'I wish Pete was here to share it. He would've loved this.'

'So would Ally,' she said softly. 'And you know what? I think they're looking down on us right now, hugging each other and saying they made exactly the right choice.'

To her surprise, he reached over to touch her cheek. 'Know what? I agree.'

Emmy felt warm all over. Right now they were definitely in accordance. And nothing felt better than this.

CHAPTER ELEVEN

Two nights later, Tyler wasn't settling in his cot as he usually did after a bath and a story; he was just grizzling and looking unhappy. It didn't look like teething, because although his cheeks were red he wasn't dribbling. Emmy laid her fingertips against his forehead and bit her lip. He felt a bit too hot for her liking.

Where was the thermometer?

She looked through the top drawer of Tyler's dressing table. Ally had shown it to her when she'd bought it. All she had to do now was put a thin plastic cone over the tip of the digital thermometer, place it in the baby's ear, and press a button.

Except she couldn't get the thermometer to switch on.

Oh, no. And she had a nasty feeling that they didn't have any spare batteries that would fit.

Although it was her night on duty, she wanted

a second opinion—especially as the thermometer was out of action.

'Shh, sweetie, we'll do something to make you
feel better,' she said, scooping the baby up and
holding him close. She carried him down to the
living room, where Dylan was working on his
laptop.

'Sorry to interrupt you,' she said, 'but I need
a second opinion.'

'What's up?' he asked.

'The thermometer battery's run out and we
don't have a spare. Does Tyler feel hot to you,
or am I just being paranoid?'

He felt the baby's forehead. 'No, he feels hot
to me, too. What do we do now? Where's the
book?' He grabbed *The Baby Bible* and looked
something up in the index. He frowned as he
swiftly read the relevant page. 'Do we have any
baby paracetamol?'

'It's in the kitchen with the medicine cabinet.'

'Good. We need to give him that to help bring
his temperature down, and while that's working we have to strip him down to his vest and
sponge him down with tepid water.' He held out
his arms for the baby. 'I'll give him a cuddle and

sing to him while you go and get the stuff. I'll meet you in the bathroom.'

The baby was still crying softly when Emmy came upstairs with the baby paracetamol and the syringe. Dylan had taken the babygro off and was rocking Tyler and singing to him.

Dylan glanced at the syringe and his eyes widened. 'What, we have to give him an injection?'

'No. The instructions say it's easier to give medicine to babies with an oral syringe than a spoon,' she explained.

'Right.'

Between them, they managed to administer the medicine, then sponged the baby with tepid water.

'Sorry, I interrupted you from your work.' She blew out a breath. 'It's my shift, and I should be able to cope. It's just… This is what keeps me awake at night. I worry about him. I worry that every cough and sneeze will turn into meningitis. That he'll die and it'll be all my fault for not looking after him properly.'

'Emmy, he doesn't have meningitis. He doesn't have a rash.'

'There isn't one at first. We could blink and

he'll be covered in purple stuff that won't go away when you press a glass against it.' She'd read all the books. She knew the signs. And she had nightmares about it. Terror that made her breathing go shallow.

'We're both keeping an eye on him, so we won't miss anything between us.' He rested his fingertips against her cheek, his touch calming her. 'Deep breaths, Emmy. He's not going to die and you're doing a great job of looking after him. And don't apologise for interrupting me.' He cradled the baby tenderly. 'He's not well, and he needs to come first. I would've done the same if it was my shift.'

'I'll get him a drink of cooled boiled water. It might help him feel better.'

'Good idea. It must be some sort of bug. There are quite a few people at work with rotten colds.' He looked stricken. 'Oh, no. I probably brought the germs home with me.'

She shook her head. 'It's not your fault, Dylan. He could have caught a virus absolutely any-where.'

Three hours later, the baby was fast asleep, but

Emmy was still worried about him. 'I think I'll sleep in his room tonight.'

'You're not going to get a lot of rest on the floor,' Dylan pointed out.

'I know.' She sighed. 'Or maybe I'll bring him in with me. Except I'm a bit scared of rolling over in the night and squishing him.'

He looked at her. 'If it was my shift tonight, you still wouldn't be able to sleep because you'd be worrying about him, right?'

'I guess so.'

'Don't take this the wrong way,' he warned, 'but maybe we could both look after him, to-night. I do trust you—of *course* I do—but this is the first time he's been ill since we've been looking after him, and it worries me.'

'Me, too,' she admitted.

'We could take two-hour shifts, so one of us stays awake and keeps an eye on him while the other of us has a nap,' he suggested

She nodded. 'But it isn't fair to keep moving him between our rooms—and, as you said, the nursery floor isn't that comfortable.' The sensi-ble course was obvious. But actually saying it... She took a deep breath. 'OK. Your bed or mine?'

Dylan gave her a rueful smile. 'I never thought I'd hear those words from you, Em.'

'Believe you me, I never thought I'd say them to you,' she said dryly. 'And this is only because we both need to look after him. I'm not coming on to you.' Though even as she said it, she felt her face flood with colour. She was horribly aware that, in another life, she *would* be coming on to Dylan—because she liked the man he'd become. And she definitely found him attractive.

Which was why she found her most frumpy pair of pyjamas before she showered, just to make the point that there was nothing sexual about this. She felt amazingly shy as she changed into her nightwear—which was ridiculous, considering that she was covered from head to toe and she knew that Dylan had seen more of her body when she was wearing a dress. Even so, she kept the bedside light on its lowest setting.

There was a knock on the door.

And how stupid that her heart missed a beat.

'Come in,' she called, hoping that her voice didn't sound as husky and nervous to him as it did to her.

He walked in wearing just a pair of pyjama bottoms, carrying the sleeping baby.

'I, um, don't tend to wear a pyjama top because I get too hot at night. Is that a problem for you?'

'No, it's fine.' She really hoped he hadn't heard that little shiver in her voice. *Too hot at night.* Oh-h-h. He looked amazingly hot right now. She could really see that he worked out at the gym regularly because his muscles were beautifully sculpted; he had good abs and strong arms, and he wouldn't have looked out of place in a perfume ad. Especially dressed the way he was, right now.

And that was totally inappropriate. He was here in her bedroom because Tyler was sick and they were sharing his care, that was all.

'Which side of the bed do you prefer to sleep on?' he asked.

'The right side—nearest the door,' she said.

'Fine by me.' He pulled the covers back and gently laid Tyler in the middle of the bed. He touched the baby's forehead and grimaced. 'He still feels hot.'

'We'd better not put a cover over him, then.'

They both climbed into bed, on either side of the baby.

'Poor little mite,' Emmy said softly. 'I wish I could have that high temperature for him.'

'Me, too,' Dylan said. 'It's weird how protective I feel about him. I never thought I'd ever feel this way about a baby.'

It was as if Tyler were their natural child, Emmy thought. She wasn't his birth mother, but she was in the position of his mother, now, and she loved him deeply. Dylan clearly felt the same way, as if he were Tyler's real father.

'We're privileged,' she said softly.

'Yes, we are.' He paused. 'Shall I take the first shift while you try to get some sleep for a couple of hours? I'll wake you when it's your turn.'

'OK. Thanks, Dylan. I appreciate the backup.'

'You'd have done the same if it'd been my turn to look after him,' he said. 'Try to get some sleep.'

She turned over so her back was to him, but she was so aware of him. He was in her bed, barely an arm's reach away. And if Tyler hadn't been there…

No, no and *no*. She was not going to allow herself to think about the possibilities.

Eventually Emmy managed to get to sleep. Then she became aware of someone stroking her arm and shaking her shoulder very gently. 'Emmy? Wake up.'

'Uhh.' It took a second for her to think why Dylan would be shaking her awake; then she remembered and sat up with a jolt. 'Is Tyler OK?'

'He's still a bit warm, but I put a single sheet over him because his legs and arms seemed a bit cold.'

'Good idea. You get some sleep now. I'll stay awake.'

Still feeling groggy, she placed her fingertips on Tyler's forehead. Dylan's assessment was spot on.

She was glad that Dylan turned his back to her to go to sleep, because she really didn't want him to catch her looking lustfully at him. Even his back was beautiful. She itched to sketch him, though it was years since she'd taken her Art A level and sketched a life model. Apart from those brief sketches she'd made of Tyler, she'd stuck mainly to abstracts and the designs for her jewellery. But Dylan was beautiful. He'd be a joy to sketch. She fixed the picture in her mind, intending to indulge herself later, then watched Tyler sleeping. The baby looked angelic with that mop of dark curls; and she was glad to see, even in the low light in the room, that his cheeks didn't look quite so red.

In his sleep, Dylan shifted to face her. In repose, he looked younger. It took Emmy a while to realise what the difference was, and then she worked it out: he didn't have that slight air of wariness she was used to.

Someone had hurt him pretty deeply, Emmy was sure. Nadine was the obvious candidate, but Emmy had a feeling that it went deeper than that. Why had he been so resistant to the idea of having a child of his own? Had he had a rotten childhood?

Not that he'd tell her, she knew. Even if she asked him straight out. He was way too private for that, and it was surprising that he'd already let this much slip to her.

Finally her two-hour watch was over. She checked Tyler's temperature again. Good. It was definitely going down. She reached over to lay a hand on Dylan's arm. His skin felt so good against her fingertips. Soft and smooth. Tempting her to explore further.

Get a grip, Emmy Jacobs, she lambasted herself silently. This isn't about you.

She patted his arm lightly, but it didn't wake him at all. She shook his shoulder, and there was still no response. Dylan was clearly in a really deep sleep. And he had taken the first shift; he must've been exhausted. She decided to leave him sleeping for another hour, then tried to wake him again. This time, she climbed out of bed and went round to his side, so she could shake him harder without waking the baby.

In response, Dylan reached out to her and mumbled something she didn't quite catch. It sounded like 'Mmm, Dee'.

'Dylan,' she said in an urgent whisper.

'Mmm,' he muttered. This time, he actually pulled her into his arms and snuggled closer.

Oh, help.

If it weren't for the baby lying next to him, she could be oh, so tempted. All she had to do was to move her head slightly and her mouth would touch against his. She could kiss him awake. See where it led them.

But he'd said 'Dee', and she had a nasty feeling that he was dreaming about his ex. Mmm, Dee. Nadine. They sounded the same, mumbled in sleep. And how stupid she was to think that Dylan would get over his wife that quickly. He was obviously still in love with his ex. Yes, there was a definite attraction between the two of them, but physical attraction wasn't enough. Her relationships never lasted. If she had a fling with Dylan, it would make everything way too complicated. She really couldn't do this.

She managed to resist the temptation—only just—and wriggled out of his arms.

'Dylan,' she said, more loudly this time.

He woke with a start and looked at her in utter confusion. Then his expression cleared as he obviously remembered where he was and why. 'How's Tyler?'

'Still a little bit warm, but nowhere near as hot as he was. He's asleep.'

'Good. Is it three o'clock?'

'Four.'

He looked shocked. 'You were supposed to wake me at three.'

'Dylan, you sleep like a log. I couldn't wake you.'

He grimaced. 'I'm sorry. OK. I'll take the next three hours and I'll wake you at seven, not six, OK?'

'OK.' She was still feeling slightly light-headed; but that had to be from lack of sleep. It had absolutely nothing to do with the way Dylan had pulled her into his arms and held her close. Did it?

Emmy looked absolutely shattered, Dylan thought—and no wonder, since her shift had lasted longer than his. He felt guilty about it, and lapsed into silence to let her sleep. He touched Tyler's forehead, just to check; she was right, the baby felt cooler.

He shifted onto his side to watch the baby. Emmy had turned away from him to sleep, but he could still feel her warmth in his arms. When she'd woken him, for a moment he'd been con-fused and thought he was back in his old house, the one he'd shared with Nadine before he'd moved into the Docklands flat. It had seemed natural to draw her closer, hold her.

Hopefully she'd forget about that by the morning. He didn't want her to think he was coming on to her, because it could make things so awkward between them. And he didn't want it to go back to the bad old days, when they hadn't got on.

Funny, sharing a house with Emmy hadn't been like sharing with Nadine, even in the early days when he and Nadine had been happy. With Emmy, he didn't feel any pressure. He didn't have anything to live up to, because they'd started from the lowest possible point and thought the worst of each other.

And these past few months had been a revelation. He'd been so sure that he didn't want a family. That he didn't want to risk things going wrong and for his child to grow up as unhappy as he'd been. Even when Nadine had given him an ultimatum, his feelings hadn't changed and he knew he'd made the right decision.

Yet, ever since he'd become a stand-in father, things had been different. Over the months, he'd grown to love his godson. He loved seeing all the little changes every day, hearing the little boy's vocabulary grow from a simple da-da, ba-ba, through to 'Dih-dih' for Dylan and 'Ehhhm,' for Emmy, and sounds that resembled real words—like the time in the butterfly house when Emmy had been convinced that he'd said 'fish'. He enjoyed seeing Tyler's anticipation as they read through a story and were about to reach his favourite bits. He enjoyed the simple clapping games Emmy had taught him to play with the little boy.

And Emmy herself...

There was the rub.

She was Tyler's stand-in mother. Dylan's co-guardian and housemate.

They were well on the way to becoming friends. He enjoyed her company, and he thought she enjoyed his, too. And, although they'd agreed to have alternate weekends off from childcare, in recent weeks they'd ended up spending a fair bit of those weekends together.

It felt like being a family. What he'd always said he didn't want. And what he'd discovered that, actually, yes, he did want. Very much indeed.

She shifted in bed, turning to face him, and he held his breath.

Spiky Emmy, the cynical and brittle woman he'd loathed so much in the past, wasn't here. This was sweet, gentle, soft Emmy. Vulnerable Emmy, who'd had her confidence chipped away by exes who couldn't see her for who she was, only what they wanted her to be. Emmy, who didn't really believe in herself.

Dylan could see her for who she was. And he liked her. More than liked her.

But could he ask her to take a chance with him—to make their unexpected family a real one?

It would be a risk. A huge risk. It had gone wrong with Nadine; he couldn't make any promises that he'd get it right, second time round, with Emmy. And he knew she shared similar fears, given that she'd been let down in the past.

Somehow he'd have to overcome those fears. Teach her that he wasn't like the men she'd dated before: that he saw her for who she was and he liked her just the way she was. And then maybe, just maybe, they'd stand a chance.

CHAPTER TWELVE

A WEEK LATER, Emmy opened the thick brown envelope that had just been delivered, to discover an early copy of the glossy magazine that had interviewed her.

'Ty, look—it's Aunty Emmy's feature,' she said, waving the magazine at him.

Tyler was much more interested in picking up the bricks they'd been playing with, and dropping them.

She built him another tower to enjoy knocking down, counting the bricks for him as she did so, then flicked through the magazine to the article. There was a nice picture of her with Tyler, and they'd really showcased her jewellery beautifully. But her delight turned to dismay as she skimmed through the text.

She'd explained the situation to the journalist. She'd made it totally clear that she and Dylan were Tyler's co-guardians and they weren't an item. So why did the article make reference to Dylan being her partner?

Oh, no. He wasn't going to be happy about that. At all.

She paced the house all morning. What was the best way to deal with this?

In the end, she decided to tell him straight. Sooner rather than later.

She waited until Tyler took his late morning nap, then called Dylan at work.

He answered immediately. 'Is Tyler all right?'

'Yes, he's fine.'

Her shakiness must've shown in her voice, because he asked, 'What's wrong?'

'There's something you need to know. It's pretty bad.' She took a deep breath. 'The magazine's coming out next week. They sent me an early copy today.'

'And they didn't use your jewellery in the end?' He sounded sympathetic. 'More fool them.'

'It's not that. They did use my pieces.' She swallowed hard. 'But they've used a picture of me with Tyler—and they've said in the piece that you're my partner. They actually named you as computer superguru Dylan Harper. And it—

well, basically it implied that Tyler's our child. I told the journalist why we were sharing a house and sharing Tyler's care. I can't believe they got it wrong like this! I'm so sorry. If this causes you any problems...' Her voice faded. If it caused him problems, she had no idea what she could do to fix it. Would it make his divorce more difficult?

'They got the wrong end of the stick. So what? It doesn't matter. Stop worrying,' he said, surprising her. She'd been so sure he'd be annoyed about it. 'The main thing is that they showcased your jewellery.'

'They did. And the jet animals.'

'Good. Now breathe, Emmy.'

'Thank you,' she said in a small voice. 'I thought you'd be livid.'

'It could be a lot worse. Most people know the press exaggerate, so don't worry about it. Just wait for people to start contacting you with commissions—and then you'll be so busy you won't have time to worry about it anymore.'

It was another week until the magazine was in the shops. Although Dylan had told her not to worry about it, Emmy still couldn't help fretting. If anyone who knew him read the piece, they'd get completely the wrong idea.

The day before the magazine came out Dylan distracted her when he called her from work.

'Don't tell me—an emergency project meeting and you're going to be late?' she asked.

'No—and I'm bringing champagne home. I got some good news this afternoon.'

'You got the Burroughs contract?'

'I certainly did.'

'Fantastic.' Emmy was genuinely pleased for him. 'Well done.'

'It was partly thanks to you,' Dylan pointed out.

'No, it's because he recognises your skill. Actually, I have some news for you. Elaine Burroughs rang. She's bringing her daughter over to see me next week.'

'For a commission? That's great. Well done. Got to go but I'll see you later. Oh—and please don't cook monkfish.'

She just laughed. 'For that, I'm ordering a takeaway. See you later.' She replaced the phone and cuddled Tyler. 'You know what? This is all starting to work out. It's not quite how Dylan and I wanted things—we'd both do anything to have your mum and dad back with us. But, as second-best goes, this is pretty good.'

Over champagne, that evening, Dylan said, 'I want to take you out to dinner to say thanks—being here with us really made a difference to Ted's decision to give us the project. Do you think your mum would babysit Ty for us?'

'Probably. I'll ask her,' Emmy said.

'Do you mind if I ask her?' Dylan asked.

She smiled. 'You know her number.' Dylan might not be that close to his own mother, she thought, but he definitely got on well with hers.

The following evening was Dylan's turn to cook. Over pasta, he told her, 'I spoke to your mum this morning. It's all arranged; we're going tomorrow.'

'Going where?' she asked.

'Out to lunch,' he said. 'Except we need to leave really early tomorrow morning, and you'll need your passport.'

She frowned. 'Why do I need my passport?'

'Don't be difficult,' he said. 'I was going to take you out to dinner, but I thought lunch might be more fun.'

'Lunch is fine, but what does that have to do with my passport?'

'Surprise.'

She sighed. 'You do know I hate surprises, don't you?'

'I think you'll like this one.' Annoyingly, he refused to be drawn on any further details.

'Are you at least going to tell me the dress code?' she asked in exasperation.

He thought about it for a moment. 'Smart casual—probably a little bit more on the smart side. You definitely need shoes you can walk in.'

'So we're walking somewhere?'

'End of information bulletin. No more answers,' he said, and gave her the most infuriating grin. Worse still, he refused to be drawn for the rest of the evening.

'I swear I'm never playing poker with you,' she said. 'You're inscrutable.'

He just laughed. 'I've been called worse.'

The next morning, Dylan knocked on Emmy's bedroom door at what felt like just before the crack of dawn. 'We're leaving in half an hour.'

Which gave her just enough time to shower, wash her hair, dress, and check in on Tyler. Her mother was already in the kitchen when Emmy came downstairs, and the kettle was on. 'Hi, Mum. Thanks for babysitting. Tyler's still asleep, given it's the crack of dawn.' She greeted her mother with a hug and kiss. 'Coffee and toast?'

'We don't have time,' Dylan said.

She gave him a sceptical look. 'You know I'm horrible if I haven't eaten. And why do we have to leave so early if we're going out to lunch, which won't be for hours?'

He answered her question with one of his own. 'You've definitely got your passport in your bag?'

She gave him a withering look. 'I'm not *that* flaky, Dylan.'

'Sorry. Old habits die hard.' He ruffled her hair. 'Let's go. We have a train to catch.'

So wherever they were going, it was by Tube. She still had no idea why he wanted her to bring her passport; though, knowing Dylan, that could be a red herring. She kissed her mum goodbye; to her surprise, so did he. Together, they headed for the Tube station, a ten-minute walk away.

Emmy noticed that although Dylan was wearing one of his work suits, teamed with a white shirt and highly polished shoes, at least for once he wasn't wearing a tie. She'd opted for a simple black shift dress teamed with black tights and flat shoes; a silver and turquoise choker; and a turquoise pashmina.

'You look lovely,' he said.

She inclined her head. 'Thank you, kind sir. Actually, you don't look so bad yourself.'

He smiled back at her. 'Why, thank you.'

Ten minutes later, they arrived at King's Cross. The second he directed her through the exit to St Pancras, she realised where they were going. 'We're going to *Paris* for lunch, Dylan? That's incredibly decadent!'

'Not really. It's as quick to take the train from London to Paris as it is to drive from London to Brighton,' he pointed out. 'Anyway, I love Paris. It's a beautiful city.'

To her delight, he'd booked them in business class so they could have breakfast on the train.

'So this is why you wouldn't let me have even a piece of toast at home,' she said, surveying the feast in front of her. Champagne with fresh orange juice, smoked salmon and scrambled egg, fresh strawberries, and good coffee. 'This has

to be the most perfect breakfast ever. I feel totally spoiled.'

He smiled. 'Good.'

'I've never been in business class before.'
Because she could only really afford standard
class. And only then if she booked the seat early
enough to get the supercheap rate.

He shrugged. 'The seats are more comfortable.'

'Thank you, Dylan. This is a real treat.'

Dylan watched her selecting what to have next;
he loved the fact that she was enjoying her food
rather than picking at it, the way Nadine always
had.

She caught him watching her. 'Sorry. Am I
being greedy?'

He laughed. 'No, I was just thinking how nice
it is that you enjoy your food instead of nibbling
on a lettuce leaf.'

'This is a lot better than you or I can cook,' she
said with a smile. 'And if we're going to Paris,
I take it we're walking, so I'm going to burn all
this off anyway.'

The journey to the Gare du Nord was quick

and uneventful; a short trip on the Métro took them to the Champs Elysées.

'It's too long since I've been to Paris. I'd almost forgotten how lovely it is—all that space in the streets, all the windows and the balconies.' She gestured across to a terrace on the other side of the street. 'I love that wrought ironwork.'

He smiled at her; he recognised that light in her eyes. The same as it had been at the butterfly house, and he'd seen drafts of designs that reminded him of the metalwork in the old Edwardian conservatory. 'Are you going to get your notebook out and start sketching?'

She smiled back. 'Not in the middle of the street. But would you mind if I took some photographs to remind me later?'

''Course not. Enjoy.'

They wandered down the street and stopped in a small café. Macaroons were arranged in a cone shape on the counter, showcasing all the different colours available, from deep pink through to browns, yellows and pistachio green.

'I guess we have to try them, as we're in Paris,' he said, and ordered macaroons with their coffee.

'This is just *lovely*. The perfect day.' Her eyes were all huge and shiny with pleasure—and that in turn made Dylan feel happy, too.

This was definitely as good as it got.

And taking her to Paris was the best idea he'd ever had. Romantic and sweet—and this might be the place where he could ask her to change their relationship. Be more than just his co-guardian. If he could find the right words.

'What would you like to do before lunch?' he asked.

'Are you planning to go somewhere in particular for lunch?'

'Yes. We need to be in the fourth arrondissement at one o'clock, but before then we can go wherever you like. I assume you'd like to go to an art gallery?'

'That's a tough one,' she said. 'Even at this time of day, I think there will be too much of a queue at the Louvre.' She looked at him. 'You said the fourth arrondissement, so that means the old quarter. Could we go to Notre Dame and see the grotesques?'

'Sure,' he said. 'I've never been. It'd be interesting to see them.' He'd visited most of the art

galleries and museums, as well as the Sacré-
Coeur and Montmartre, but he'd never actually
been to Notre Dame.

'It's a bit of a trek up the tower,' she warned.

'I don't mind. I know you said you wanted to
walk, but how do you feel about going by river?'

She nodded. 'That works for me. I love boat
trips.'

He made a mental note; it might be nice to take
Tyler to Kew on the river, in the spring.

When they'd finished their coffee, they took
the Batobus along the Seine to the Île de la Cité,
with Emmy exclaiming over several famous
buildings on the way. They walked up the steps
from the bridge, then across the square with the
famous vista of Notre Dame and its square dou-
ble tower and rose window. The stone of the cathedral looked brilliant white against the blue
sky.

'I love the shape of the rose window, the way
it fans out—almost like the petals of a gerbera
crossed with a spiderweb,' she said.

'Are you thinking a pendant?' he asked.

She nodded. 'Do you mind if I take some pictures?'

He laughed. 'You really don't have to ask me every time, Emmy. Just do it. Today's for you to enjoy.'

'Thank you.' She took several photos on her phone, and then they queued at the side of the cathedral to walk up the tower to the galleries.

'I always think of poor Quasimodo, here,' Emmy said. 'So deeply in love with Esmeralda, yet afraid she'll despise him like everyone else does.'

'So you cried over the film?'

'No, over the book,' she said, surprising him.

'You read Victor Hugo?' He hadn't expected that.

She looked at him. 'It was one of my set texts for A level.'

'English?'

'French,' she corrected.

He blinked. 'You let everyone think you're this ditzy designer, but you're really bright, aren't you?'

'Don't sound so surprised. It kind of spoils the compliment.' She rolled her eyes. 'I'm really going to have to make you that jet rhino, aren't I?'

'Hey.' He gave her a brief hug. 'I didn't mean it like that. But you do keep your light under a bushel.'

'Maybe.'

They walked up the hundreds of spiral steps; the stone was worn at the edges where thousands of people had walked up those steps before them. At the first stage, they had amazing views of the square and the Seine, with the Eiffel Tower looming in the background. They carried on up to the next stage and saw the famous chimera grotesques in the Grande Galerie. Dylan was fascinated by the pelican. 'And that elephant would look great carved in jet,' he said.

'For Ty's Noah's Ark? Good idea,' she said.

'So why are the gargoyles here?' he asked.

'Strictly speaking, gargoyles carry rainwater away from the building. These ones don't act as conduits; they're just carvings, so they're called grotesques. These are Victorian ones, done at the same time as the restoration. And there's a fabulous legend—see the one sitting over there, looking over the Seine?'

'Yes.'

'Apparently it watches out for people who are drowning, then swoops down and rescues them.'

He raised an eyebrow. 'Is that something else you learned for your A level?'

'No. Actually, I can't even remember where I heard it, but I think it's a lovely story.'

Emmy liked the brighter side of life, he noticed. Trust her to know about that sort of legend.

They walked across to the other tower to see the bell, then back down all the steps.

'Did you want to go inside the cathedral?' he asked.

'Yes, please. I love the stained glass,' she said.

As he'd half expected, she took several photographs of the rose window with its beautiful blue and red glass.

'Is this a Victorian renovation, too?' he asked.

'Most of this one's original thirteenth-century glass. If I were you, I'd tell me to shut up, now,' she said with a grin, 'because stained glass was one of the modules in my degree, and Ally says I get really boring about it, always dragging her off to tiny churches to see rare specimens.' Her smile faded. 'Said,' she corrected herself.

He took her hand and squeezed it. 'You really miss her, don't you?'

'Yes. But I'm glad we have Tyler. We'll see her and Pete in him as he grows up.'

And then he forgot to release her hand. She didn't make a protest; it was only as they strolled through the streets of the old quarter that he realised he was still holding her hand. And that he was actually *happy*. Happier than he could remember being for a long, long time.

Maybe he didn't need to struggle with words, after all. Maybe all he had to do was *be*.

She insisted on stopping at one of the stalls and buying a baby-sized beret for Tyler. She gave him a sidelong look. 'I'm tempted to get you one as well.'

'You expect me to wear a beret?' he scoffed.

'Mmm, and you could have a Dali moustache to go with it.'

He shuddered. 'What next, a stripy jumper and a red scarf?'

She laughed. 'OK, so a beret is a bit too avant-garde for you—but men can look good in a beret, you know.'

'I think I'll pass,' he said. 'Though I admit Tyler will look cute.'

As they crossed the bridge she asked, 'Where are we going?'

'Time for lunch,' he said.

They stopped outside a restaurant in the old quarter right next to the Seine with view of Notre Dame. She looked at him, wide-eyed. 'I know of this place. Zola, Dumas and de Maupassant all used to come here—it's hideously expensive, Dylan. It's Michelin starred.'

And it had a great reputation, which was why he'd booked it. He simply shrugged. 'They might have monkfish.'

She let the teasing comment pass. 'I've never eaten in a restaurant with a Michelin star.'

'Good. That means you'll enjoy this,' he said.

Enjoy?

This was way, way out of her experience. Dylan, despite the fact that he wasn't keen on cooking, clearly liked good food and was used to eating at seriously swish restaurants like this one.

Enjoy.

OK. She'd give it a go. Even if she did feel a bit intimidated.

The maître d' showed them to a table in a private salon. She'd never been to such an amazing place before; the décor was all gilded wood and hand-painted wallpaper. There was a white damask cloth on the table along with lit white candles and silverware, and gilded Louis XIV chairs. The windows were covered with dark voile curtains, making the room seem even more intimate. And the maître d' told them that the waiter would be along whenever they rang the bell.

Emmy's eyes met Dylan's as they were seated. For a moment, she allowed herself to think what it would be like if this were a proper romantic date. A total sweep-you-off-your-feet date.

He'd held her hand as they'd wandered through the city together; so was this Dylan's way of taking her on a date without having to ask her? He didn't like emotional stuff, so she knew he'd shy away from the words; but this definitely felt like more than a thank you. More like the fact that he wanted to be with her. Some time for just the two of them. Together.

Unless she was projecting her own wants on him and seeing what she wanted to see…

When she looked at her menu, she noticed that there were no prices. In her experience, this meant the food was seriously expensive. And it made her antsy.

She coughed. 'Dylan, there aren't any prices on my menu.'

He spread his hands. 'And?'

She bit her lip. 'I'm used to paying my way.'

'Not on this occasion. I'm taking you out to lunch to say thank you.'

So not a date, then. She tried not to feel disappointed.

'Just as you took me out to dinner,' he reminded her.

'But when I took you out, it wasn't somewhere as swish as this.'

He sighed. 'Emmy, if you're worrying about the bill, then please don't. I can afford this. My business is doing just fine—and, thanks to this new contract, it's going to be doing even better. I couldn't have got this contract without your help, so please let me say thank you.'

'Can I at least buy the wine?' she asked.

'No. This one is all on me. And, I don't know about you, but I've got to the stage where I fall asleep if I drink at lunchtime, so I was going to suggest champagne by the glass.' His eyes crinkled at the corners. 'But I might let you buy me a crêpe later.'

A crêpe. Which would only cost a couple of Euros, whereas she was pretty sure the bill here was going to be nearer half a month's mortgage payment for her. 'I feel really guilty about this.'

'Don't. I'm doing it because I want to treat you. So enjoy it. What would you like for lunch?'

Protesting any more would be churlish. Emmy scanned the menu. 'It's all so fantastic, I don't know what to choose. I'm torn between lobster and asparagus.'

'We could,' he said, 'order both—and share them.'

Now it was starting to feel like a date again. And that made her all quivery inside. 'Sounds good,' she said.

She actually enjoyed sharing forkfuls of starter with him. Especially as it gave her an excuse to look at his mouth as much as she liked. And she noticed he was looking at her mouth, too. As if he wanted to kiss away a stray crumb and make her forget the rest of the meal.

Oh, help. She really had to keep a lid on this.

After that, she had crayfish with satay and lime, and he chose lamb.

'Look at this. It's beautifully cooked and beautifully presented,' she said. 'I can see exactly why they have a Michelin star. This is *sublime*.'

He chuckled, and she narrowed her eyes at him. 'What's so funny?'

'That you're such a foodie—and, um, in the kitchen…'

She rolled her eyes. 'Yeah, yeah. I'm never going to live that monkfish down. You'll still tease me about it when we're ninety.'

Oh, help. Had she really said that? Implied that they were going to be together forever and ever?

'Yes. I will,' he said softly, and it suddenly made it hard for her to breathe.

She fell back on teasing. Just to defuse the intensity before she said something really, really clueless. 'I could point out that this is a bit of a pots and kettles conversation, given that you're clearly a foodie and you're about the same as I am in the kitchen.'

He laughed. 'I admit my monkfish would've been just as terrible. But you're right. This is sublime. Try it.' He offered her a forkful of lamb.

'Mmm. And try this.' She offered him some crayfish.

'So are you going to tell me that lunch in Paris was the best idea ever?' he prompted.

'That,' she said, 'depends on the dessert.'

They scanned the menu when they'd finished. 'How can you not order madeleines in France?' she asked with a smile.

'When there's chocolate soufflé on the menu,' he retorted, and she laughed.

Again they shared tastes of each other's pudding, and she enjoyed making him lean over to reach the spoon—especially when he retaliated and did likewise.

'That was fantastic,' she said when the meal was over. 'A real treat. I admit, yes, it's the best idea ever. Thank you so much.'

'My pleasure. I enjoyed it, too.'

And his smile reached his eyes; he wasn't just being polite.

They spent the rest of the afternoon browsing

in little boutiques. Again, he held her hand; and again, neither of them commented on it.

Emmy bought a box of shiny macaroons for her mother. 'And I think we should go to a toy shop, so we can bring something more than just a beret back for Ty.'

Dylan smiled. 'He probably hasn't even noticed we're gone. Unless that's just a flimsy excuse for toy shopping, Ms Jacobs.'

'It's a really flimsy excuse,' she said with a grin. 'I love toy shops.'

'I'd already noticed that,' he said, 'given how much Tyler's toy box seems to have grown recently.' He checked on his phone to find the nearest toy shop, and when they looked along the shelves Emmy was thrilled to discover a soft plush teddy bear with a beret and stripy shirt. 'This is perfect,' she said, and gave Dylan an arch look. 'Beret and stripy shirt. Hmm.'

He laughed. 'Don't you dare call it Dylan.'

'Spoilsport,' she teased.

'You know, we'll have to bring Ty to Paris when he's a little older. He'll love seeing the Eiffel Tower sparkle at night,' Dylan said.

Making plans for the future, she thought. Neither of them had said it. This was too new, too fragile. But she was beginning to think that there was a future…

When they'd finished shopping, Dylan allowed Emmy to buy him a coffee before they headed back to the Gare du Nord to catch the train to London.

Back in London, Emmy shivered when they came out of the Tube station and pulled her pashmina closer round her. 'I wish I'd brought a proper coat with me, now. It's colder than I expected.'

'Have my jacket,' he offered, starting to shrug it off.

'No, because then you'll be cold. And it's only a few minutes until we get home.'

'I'll call a taxi.'

'By the time it gets here, we could've walked home,' she pointed out.

'OK. Then let's do it this way.' He put his arm round her shoulders, drawing her close to him.

Oh, help. Her skin actually tingled where he touched her. And the whole thing sent her brain into such a flutter that she couldn't utter a word until he opened the front door and ushered her inside.

Her mum greeted them warmly. 'Did you have a good time?'

'The best,' Emmy said. 'Oh, and these are for you.' She handed her mother the bag from the patisserie. 'How's Tyler?'

'Asleep, and he's been absolutely fine all day.' She hugged them both. 'I'll call you tomorrow.'

'Thanks for babysitting for us.' Dylan hugged her back. 'I only had one glass of champagne at lunchtime, so I'm OK to drive. I'll run you home.'

'That's sweet of you.'

Emmy checked on Tyler while Dylan drove her mother home.

Today had been magical. The way Dylan had fed her morsels from his plate at lunchtime, and walked through Paris hand in hand with her; the way he'd automatically offered her his jacket and then, when she'd refused, put his arm round her to keep her warm... Was she adding two and two and making five, or was it the same for him? Had they become something more than co-guardians? Was this a real relationship—one for keeps?

Dylan was back by the time she came downstairs.

'Everything OK?' he asked.

'Tyler's fine. Thank you for today. It really was special.' She stood up, intending to kiss his cheek. But somehow she ended up brushing her mouth against his instead.

She pulled back and looked up at him.

His eyes were intense, darkened from their normal cornflower-blue to an almost stormy navy. She shivered, and couldn't help looking at his mouth again.

He leaned forward and touched his mouth to hers in the lightest, sweetest kiss. Automatically, she parted her lips and tipped her head back in offering. He drew her closer and she could feel the lean, hard strength of his body. So much for Dylan being a geek; he felt more like the athlete she'd once dated, all muscular. And she couldn't help remembering the way he'd looked in her bed, half-naked and asleep.

Her hands were tangled in his hair and his arms were wrapped tightly round her as he deepened the kiss. Her head was spinning, and it felt as if the room were lit by a hundred stars.

He shuddered as he broke the kiss. 'Emmy.'

'I know.' She reached up to trace his lower lip with the tip of her forefinger.

'Are we going to regret this in the morning?' he asked, his voice huskier this time.

'I don't know. Maybe not.' She shivered as he drew the tip of her forefinger into his mouth and sucked; she closed her eyes and tipped her head back, inviting another kiss.

He released her hand. 'Emmy. My common sense is deserting me. If you don't tell me to stop…' he warned.

Then she knew what was going to happen.

And every nerve in her body longed for it.

She opened her eyes and looked at him. 'Yes.'

Still holding her gaze, he scooped her up and carried her up the stairs.

CHAPTER THIRTEEN

EMMY LAY IN the dark, curled against Dylan.

Are we going to regret this in the morning?
His words from earlier echoed in her head.

Would they?

Part of her regretted it already. Because she was scared that now everything could go *really* wrong. When had she ever managed to make a relationship last? When had she ever picked the right man? What if Dylan changed his mind about her?

'I can almost hear you thinking,' he said softly, stroking her hair.

'Panicking,' she admitted. 'Dylan—I'm not good at this stuff. I've messed up every relationship I've ever had.'

'You're good at picking Mr Wrong,' he said. 'And you think I might be another.' He shifted so he could brush his mouth against hers. 'Maybe I'm not.'

She swallowed hard. 'I swore I'd never risk anything like this again, not after the last time.'

'What happened? He was another one who wanted you to change?'

'No,' she said miserably. 'Far worse. I should've told you before. He was married.' She grimaced. 'Finding out that I was the other woman...I hated myself for that.'

'You didn't know?'

'No. Especially after what happened to my mum, no way would I ever have tried to break up a family like that. I found out when I called his mobile phone and his wife answered.' Her breath hitched. 'I wasn't the first. Far from it. But I felt so horrible that I'd done that to some-one. My mum was devastated when my father had affairs; and I felt like the lowest of the low for making someone else feel like that.'

'It's not your fault if he lied to you,' Dylan pointed out. He sighed. 'Though I don't have room to talk, do I? Technically, I'm married.'

'You've been separated for months, and you're just waiting for that last bit of paper to come through. That's totally different. You've been honest with me. He wasn't. Though I should've worked it out for myself,' Emmy said. 'Afterwards, when I thought about it, it was really obvious. We always went to my place rather than his, and he never stayed overnight. If we did go out, we only ever went to obscure places, and half the time we'd have to call it off—he said it was because of work, but it was obviously because he was doing family things. I should've seen it.'

'It wasn't your fault,' Dylan said again. 'You wouldn't have had anything to do with him if you'd known he was married. He was the cheat, not you.' He sighed. 'And his wife…maybe she loved him very much, but it's still a shame that she'd let herself be treated like that. It sounds to me as if she deserved better. And so do you.'

'I don't know, Dylan. Sometimes my judgement is atrocious.'

'Mine, too,' he said. 'But it's late, we've had a long day, and now maybe isn't the best time to talk. Go to sleep, Em.' He drew her closer.

Well, at least he hadn't walked away, she thought.

Yet.

* * *

The next morning, Emmy was dimly aware of crying. *Loud* crying, which was turning into screams.

She sat up, suddenly wide awake. Tyler. She hadn't put the baby listener on last night. Because she'd...

Oh, no.

She looked at the other side of her bed.

Where Dylan was also sitting up. Completely naked. And looking shocked, embarrassed and awkward.

That made two of them. They'd complicated things hugely, last night. How were they ever going to fix this?

She glanced at the clock: half past nine. A good two and a half hours later than they were usually up. No wonder Tyler was crying. She'd missed her Pilates class. And Dylan would be lucky to get to the office on time for a meeting she knew he had this morning.

'Oh, my God. We're really late,' she said. 'And Tyler's screaming.'

Dylan looked at her. 'Emmy, we need to talk about this, but—'

'You have a meeting, and I need to feed Tyler.'

'I feel bad about leaving without…' He grimaced.

'We'll talk about it later,' she said. 'Can you close your eyes for a moment?' It was ridiculous, she knew, considering they'd both explored each other's bodies in considerable detail the night before; but she felt shy and exposed.

He mumbled something, clearly feeling as embarrassed as she did, and closed his eyes; she fled to the door, grabbed her bathrobe, and put it on as she raced to the baby's room.

And hopefully by the time she and Dylan talked, she would've rediscovered her common sense and worked out how they could deal with this with the minimum fallout for Tyler.

She scooped Tyler out of his cot and held him close. 'OK, babe, Aunty Emmy and Uncle Dylan messed up. But we'll fix things.' And they would fix things, because they didn't have any other option. 'Come on, let's get you some breakfast.'

The crying subsided, and Tyler was back to being all smiles and gurgled after she'd fed him his usual baby porridge and some puréed apple, and given him some milk.

Dylan was clearly as glad as she was of the respite, because she didn't see him at all before he left the house.

She put Tyler back in his cot with some toys to keep him amused, while she had a shower and dressed. Then she scooped him back out of his cot, changed him, and took him downstairs to play.

'I might've just made the biggest mistake of my life, Ty,' she said. 'Or it might've been the best idea ever. Right now, I just don't know.' And it terrified her. She'd already made too many mistakes. 'I don't know how Dylan really feels about me. But we both love you.' She was sure about that. 'And, whatever happens between us, we'll make sure that your world stays safe and secure and happy.'

She still didn't have any solutions by the time that Tyler had his morning nap.

And then a mobile phone shrilled. It wasn't her ringtone, so the phone must be Dylan's. He'd obviously left it behind and was probably ringing to find out where he'd left it.

She found the phone and picked it up, intending to answer and tell him yes, he'd left it here, and yes, she could drop it in to the office if he needed it. It wasn't his name on the screen; but she recognised it immediately. *Nadine.*

What should she do?

This might be important. She ought to answer it. On the other hand, if she answered the phone and Nadine demanded to know who she was, or got the wrong idea, it could make everything much more complicated.

She grabbed the landline and rang Dylan. 'You left your mobile behind.'

He groaned. 'Sorry. Well, don't think you have to bring it out to me or anything. I'll manage without it for today.'

'You might not be able to. Um, Nadine just rang.'

'Why?' He sounded shocked. 'What did she say?'

'I don't know. When I saw her name, I was too much of a coward to answer. Sorry.'

'It's fine. Probably just as well.' He sighed. 'Did she leave a message?'

She glanced at the screen of his phone. 'It looks like it.'

'What does it say?'

'How would I know? I don't listen in to your messages, Dylan.'

'It's probably something to do with paperwork for the divorce,' he said, and sighed. 'I'll sort it out. And I'll see you later. Em…'

'Yes?'

'Never mind. We'll talk when I get home.'

Emmy spent the morning playing with Tyler. But when the baby had a nap, she looked a few things up on the Internet. And then she really wished that she'd let it go. Now she'd seen a picture of Nadine, she could see that Dylan's ex was perfect for him. Poised, sleekly groomed, very together—everything that Emmy wasn't.

And the divorce was taking a very long time to come through. Assuming that they'd split up before Tyler was born…why hadn't it been settled yet? Did Nadine want him back? Had she heard from a colleague that Dylan was guardian to the baby she'd wanted, and did she think that Dylan might be prepared to give their marriage another chance?

She blew out a breath. OK. Dylan wasn't a liar and a cheat. He wouldn't have slept with her if he'd still been in love with his ex. She knew that.

But...

Her relationships always went wrong. What was to say that this would be any different? And there had been that night where he'd pulled her close and murmured Nadine's name...

The doubts flooded through her, and she just couldn't shift them. What if Dylan had changed his mind about her? What if, when he came home tonight, he wanted them to go back to their old relationship—at arm's length and only sharing the baby's care? What if they got together and, once the first flush of desire had worn off, he started realising how many flaws she had, just as her exes always had? What if he started wanting her to change, and she couldn't be who he wanted her to be?

Tyler woke; feeding him distracted her for a little bit, but still the thoughts whizzed round her head. And the doubts grew and grew and grew until she felt suffocated by them.

'I need to think about this,' she told the baby. 'I need to work out what I want. Find out what Dylan wants. And I think we need to be apart while we work it out.'

She knew exactly where she could go. Where

she'd be welcomed, where the baby would be fussed over, where she'd be able to walk for miles next to the sea. Where she could talk to someone clear-sighted who'd listen and let her work it out.

She rang her great-aunt to check that it was convenient for her to visit, then packed swiftly. 'We're going to the sea,' she told the baby, who cooed at her and clapped his hands. 'Where I used to go when I was tiny. You'll like it.'

Then she picked up the phone again. It was only fair to tell Dylan what she planned. Except he was unavailable, in a meeting with a client. This wasn't the kind of thing she wanted to leave in a message, and she could hardly text him because his mobile phone was still here.

But she could leave him a voicemail.

She dialled his mobile number swiftly and waited for the phone to click through to his voicemail. 'Dylan, I need some space to think about things,' she said. 'To get my head straight. I'm staying at Great-Aunt Syb's. I'll text you when I get there so you know we've arrived safely.' Given what had happened to Ally and

Pete, she would've wanted him to text her if he'd been the one travelling. It was only fair.

Honestly, Dylan thought, if you were going to leave a message on someone's voicemail, you could at least make sure you were around to accept the return call.

On the third attempt, he finally got through to Nadine. 'You wanted to talk to me,' he said.

'Yes. I saw that article in the magazine.'

'Uh-huh.'

'And Jenny at the office said you were looking after Pete's son since the accident.'

Where was she going with this? He had a nasty feeling about it. 'My godson. Yes.'

She dragged in a breath. 'So you're a dad.'

Uh-oh. This was exactly what he'd thought she wanted to talk to him about. 'A stand-in one.'

'So we could—'

'No,' he cut in gently before she could finish her suggestion. 'Nadine, you're seeing someone else.'

'On the rebound from you. I still love you, Dylan. We can stop the divorce going through.

All you have to do is say yes. We can make a family together.'

'It's not quite the same thing, Nadine. You wanted a baby of your own,' he reminded her.

'And we still can. We can have a brother or sister for Tyler.'

'No. Nadine, it's over,' he said, as gently as he could. 'I'm sorry.'

'So you're really—' she took a deep breath '—with that jeweller?'

'I am,' he confirmed. And it shocked him how good that made him feel. Tonight, he'd leave the office and go home to Emmy and Tyler. His partner and his child. His unexpected family.

Her voice wobbled. 'What does she have that I don't?'

'That isn't a fair conversation,' he said. 'You're very different. Opposites, even. But she complements me. And it works.' He paused. 'Be happy, Nadine. And try to be happy for me. We've both got a chance to make a new life now, to get what we wanted.'

'I wanted it with you.'

'I'm sorry,' he said, guilt flooding through

him. 'But there's no going back for us. I know that now. We wouldn't make each other happy.'

'We could try.' Hope flared in her voice.

'I'm sorry,' he said again. 'Goodbye, Nadine. And good luck.' He cut the connection.

And now he could go home. See Emmy. Tell her that everything was going to be just fine.

Except, when he opened the front door, he realised that the house was empty.

Maybe she'd taken Tyler to the park or something. He tried calling her mobile phone from the house landline, but there was no answer. Maybe she was somewhere really noisy and hadn't heard the phone, or maybe she was in the middle of a nappy change. 'It's me. I'm home,' he said when the line clicked through to voicemail. 'See you later.'

He went in search of his mobile phone. Emmy had left it in the middle of the kitchen table. He flicked into the first screen, intending to check his text messages, and noticed that he had two voicemail messages. The first was Nadine's from earlier, asking him to call. He sighed and deleted it.

The second was probably work. He'd sneak

some in until Emmy got home, and then—well. Then he could kiss her stupid, for starters.

He smiled at the thought, and listened to the message.

And then his smile faded.

I need some space.

Uh-oh. That wasn't good. Did that mean she'd changed her mind about what had happened between them? That she didn't want to be with him?

Or had he been right about her all along and she was like his mother, unable to stick to any decisions and dropping everything at a moment's notice to go off and 'find herself'?

Feeling sick, he listened to the rest of the message.

So she was going up north. To the sea. That figured. And she'd left the message two hours ago, so right now she was probably in the car. Of course she wouldn't answer while she was driving. She'd never put Tyler at risk like that.

OK. He'd talk to her when she got there. And in the meantime he'd get on with some work.

Though it was almost impossible to concentrate. The house just didn't feel right without her and Tyler. Going for a run didn't take his mind off things, either, and nor did his shower afterwards. And he was even crosser with himself when he saw the text from Emmy when he got out of the shower. *Here safely. E.*

Just his luck that she'd texted when he wouldn't hear it. He called her back immediately, but a recorded voice informed him that the phone was unavailable. Switched off? Or was she in an area with a poor signal?

'Leave a message, or send a text,' the recorded voice told him.

Right.

'Emmy, call me. Please. We need to talk.' They really had to sort this out. Did she want him, or didn't she?

Except she didn't call him.

And Dylan was shocked to find out how much he missed them both. How much he wanted them home safely with him.

Maybe she wanted space because she wasn't sure of him. Maybe he hadn't made her realise exactly how he felt about her. Maybe she needed something from him that he wasn't good at— emotional stuff. The right words.

Maybe his mother went to find herself because she had nobody to find her. But Emmy
had someone to find *her*. She had him. And he
needed to tell her that.

It was too late to drive to Whitby now. It'd be
stupid o'clock in the morning before he got there.
But he could go and find her tomorrow. Tell her
how he felt. And hope that she'd agree to come
back with him.

First, though, where did Syb live? He had a
feeling that if he did manage to get through to
Emmy's phone to ask for the address, she'd come
up with an excuse. And this was too important
to put off. He needed to see her *now*.

Knowing Emmy, all her contacts would be on
her phone rather than written down somewhere.
But he knew she was savvy enough to keep a
backup. If she had a password on her computer
at all, he reasoned, it would be an easy one to
crack. He switched on the machine, waited for
the programs to load, and typed in Tyler's birth-
date when the computer prompted him for a
password.

Bingo.

It was a matter of seconds to find Syb's address in Emmy's contacts file. He made a note of the address for his GPS system and shut down the computer.

Tomorrow—he just hoped that tomorrow would see his life getting back on track. Back where he belonged.

CHAPTER FOURTEEN

AT FIVE O'CLOCK the next morning, Dylan gave up trying to get back to sleep. He had a shower, chugged down some coffee, and headed for Whitby.

He'd connected his phone to the car and switched it into hands-free mode, so he was able to call his second in command on his way up north to brief him on the most urgent stuff he had scheduled for the day. And, with that worry off his mind, it let him concentrate on Emmy.

As he drove over the Yorkshire moors the heather looked resplendently purple, and there was a huge rainbow in the sky. When he was small, his grandmother used to tell him there was a pot of gold at the end of a rainbow. Well, he didn't want gold. He wanted something much more precious: he wanted Emmy and Tyler.

At last he could see the sea and the spooky gothic ruin of Whitby Abbey that loomed over the town. Almost there. He didn't want to turn up empty-handed, so he stopped at a petrol station to refuel and buy flowers for both Emmy and her great-aunt. He managed to find a parking space near the house; when he rang the doorbell and waited, his heart was beating so hard that he was sure any passers-by could hear it. Finally, the door was opened by an elderly lady. 'Yes?'

'Would you be Emmy's great-aunt Syb?' he asked.

She looked wary. 'Who wants to know?'

'My name's Dylan Harper,' he said.

'Ah. So *you're* Dylan.'

Emmy had obviously talked to her great-aunt about him. And probably not in glowing terms, either. He took a deep breath. 'Please, may I see her?'

'I'm afraid she's not here.'

His heart stopped for a moment. OK, so she'd probably guess that he'd lose patience with the situation and come to see her, but surely she hadn't disappeared already? 'Where is she?' he asked.

'Walking by the sea. I told her to leave Tyler

with me—she needed some fresh air and time to think. It's hard to think when you're looking after a baby.'

'Is he OK?'

'He's absolutely fine and he's having a nap, so don't worry. Just go and find her. She'll be on the east foreshore.' He must've looked as mystified as he felt, because Syb added, 'Head for the Abbey, then instead of going up the steps just keep going forward until you get to the beach, then hug the cliffs and keep heading to the right. You'll see her.'

'Thank you.' He thrust the flowers at her. 'These are for you—well, one bunch is. The other's for Emmy.'

'Thank you, Dylan,' Syb said gently.

A cheap bunch of flowers. How pathetic was he? And the only other thing he had to give Emmy was his heart. Which was incredibly scary. What if she rejected him? What if she was here because she was trying to work out how to tell him that it was a huge mistake and she didn't want to be with him in that way? 'I, um...'

'Go and find her,' Syb said. 'Talk to her. Sort

it out between you. I'm here for Tyler, so don't rush. Take your time.'

As Dylan walked through the town he felt sick. What if she wouldn't talk to him, wouldn't listen to what he had to say? What if she didn't want him?

There were a few families on the beach, and his stomach clenched as he saw them. That was exactly what he wanted—to be able to do simple things like building a sandcastle on the beach with Tyler, and playing with him and Emmy at the edge of the sea. Family things. A *forever* family.

Please let her listen to him.

There were a few people beachcombing on the foreshore; some had hammers and chisels, and Dylan assumed they were collecting fossils. Then he rounded a corner and saw her. She bent down to pick up something from the sand; probably some jet, he thought. Syb had sent Emmy out to do something to soothe her soul, and he already knew how much she loved the sea.

He quickened his pace and nearly slipped on the treacherous surface; he blew out a breath and picked his way more steadily over towards her.

She looked up as he reached her side. 'What are you doing here?'

'I've come to see you. Talk to you.' He took a deep breath. 'Emmy, I'm good at business words and computer code and geek. I'm rubbish at the emotional stuff. I know I'm going to make a mess of this, but...' His voice faded.

She nodded. 'What did Nadine want? Was it about the paperwork?'

'No. She'd seen the article.'

'You said she wanted a baby. You have a baby, now.' Her voice wobbled. 'Is that what she wants?'

He knew with blinding clarity what she was really asking. Was that what he wanted, too? 'I'm not going to lie to you, Emmy,' he said softly. 'She did suggest it. But I said no. Because that's not what I want.'

She bit her lip. 'You don't want a child.'

He squirmed. There was no way out of this. He was going to have to bare his heart to her, even though he hated making himself that vulnerable. 'Not with her. We're not right for each other.' He dragged in a breath. 'I guess that's something else you need to know. I didn't want a child,' he said slowly, 'because of the way I grew up.'

She waited. And eventually the words flooded in to fill the silence.

'I never knew who my dad was. My mum used to go off to "find herself" every time she broke up with whoever she was dating, and she always dumped me on the nearest relative. Usually my grandparents.' He looked away. 'My grandmother loved me and had time for me but my grandfather always made me feel I was a nuisance and a burden.'

She reached out and linked her fingers through his; it gave him the strength to go on, and he looked back at her.

'I hated it. I hated feeling that I was always in the way. Then, as I grew older, I was scared that maybe I wouldn't be able to bond with a child because my parental role models were—well, not what I would've chosen myself. I was scared that I wouldn't be any good as a parent, and I never wanted a child to feel the way I did when I grew up, so I decided that I was never going to have children.' He blew out a breath. 'I suppose I married Nadine because I thought she was safe. Because I thought she wanted the same thing that I did, that her job was enough for her. But then she changed her mind about what she wanted and I just couldn't change with her. I couldn't give her what she wanted, because I was too selfish. Because I was a coward. Because I was scared I'd fail at it, and I walked away rather than trying to make it work.'

'And yet you stepped up to the mark when Ty needed you,' Emmy said softly.

'I didn't have a clue what I was doing. I still don't,' he confessed wryly.

'Me, neither—but we're muddling through, and Ty definitely feels loved and settled.' She paused. 'Is that why you didn't like me? Because you thought I was flaky and selfish and just thought of myself, like your mum? Because my relationships never lasted and Ally always had to pick up the pieces?'

He bit his lip. 'I was wrong about that. But—yes, I admit, I did.'

She sighed. 'I don't blame you. I probably would've thought the same, in your shoes.' She paused. 'Is that why you think I went away? To find myself?'

'You said you needed space. Time to think.' He paused. 'I think my mum went away to find herself, because there wasn't anyone to find her.' He looked her straight in the eye. 'But I came to find you, Emmy.'

She dragged in a breath. 'I'd never dump Ty on anyone. The only reason he's with Syb is because he's asleep—and I have my mobile phone with me. She promised to call me the second he woke up, if I wasn't already back by then.'

'I know,' he said softly. 'She told me to take our time. To talk. She's wise, your great-aunt.'

She nodded.

'So why did you leave?'

'Because I was scared,' she admitted. 'I had doubts.'

'Doubts about me, or doubts about being with me?'

'I was scared that things would change. Scared that you'd compare me to Nadine and find me wanting.' She looked anguished. 'I always pick the wrong guy. It starts off well, I think it's going to work—and then I find out that there are things he doesn't like about me. Things he expects me to change. And you used to loathe me.'

Hope flooded through him. She didn't have doubts about being with him; what she doubted was herself. Which meant she needed total honesty from him. 'Yes, I used to loathe you. But that was before I knew you properly. I don't loathe you now. And I don't want to change you, Emmy. I don't want to change a single thing.' He drew her hand to his mouth and kissed it. 'I'm sorry. I should've cancelled my meeting yesterday morning and talked to you, instead.'

'You couldn't. You were late, and it was important.'

'I never thought I'd ever say this to anyone, but I don't care if it was important. You're more important to me than work,' he said.

She stared at him, as if not quite daring to believe that he meant it.

'I should've stayed with you. Better still, instead of telling you to go to sleep, the night before, I should've talked to you about what happened between us. Listened to you. Soothed your worries, and asked you to soothe mine. But I'm rubbish at the emotional stuff, so I bailed out on you. I thought it'd give me time to work out what to say.'

'Did it?'

'No,' he admitted. 'I still don't know what to say. Or how to say it without it coming out all wrong. But...' He took a deep breath. 'My world doesn't feel right without you in it.' His heart was racing. Had he got this wrong? This could all implode, become so messy. But he owed it to their future to take that risk. 'I love you, Emmy.'

Hope blossomed in her expression. 'You love me?'

'I don't know when it happened. Or how. Or why. I just know I do. And Paris clinched it for me. I finally got why they call it the City of Light. Because you were there with me, and I was so happy.' He took a deep breath. 'It isn't the same thing I felt with Nadine. You're not safe, like I thought she was. I'm not entirely sure what makes you tick. I think we're always going to have fights—you're going to think I'm stuffy and I'm going to think you're flaky. But that's OK. We can agree to disagree. What I do know is that I love you. I want to be with you. And I want you, me and Tyler to be a proper family.

Maybe we could have a little brother or sister for him. If you…' He broke off. 'Sorry. That's too much pressure. I never expected to feel like this. I've made a mess of one marriage. I can't guarantee I'll get it right with you. But I'll try. Believe me, I'll try.'

She reached up and stroked his face. 'Dylan. I'm rubbish at relationships, too. It scares me that everything's going to go wrong.'

'But maybe it won't. Not if you want me the way I want you.'

'I do.'

'Are you sure?' She'd already walked away from him.

'I've worked you out, now. You're a goalpost shifter,' Emmy said. 'You never think you're good enough—and that's not your fault, it's because your mum's as selfish as my dad and she made you feel you weren't good enough. Except you are good enough. You *are*. You've got the biggest heart. And I…' She swallowed hard. 'I love you too, Dylan. So the answer's yes. Yes, I want to make you, me and Dylan a forever family. Yes, if we're blessed and when Ty's a little bit older, it might be nice to have another baby.' She smiled. 'We might even have more of a clue what we're doing as parents, the second time round.'

The trickle of hope became a flood. He dropped to one knee, not caring that the foreshore was rocky and slippery and wet. 'Emmy Jacobs, I know I ought to wait for that piece of paper to come through before I ask you, but I can't. I want the rest of my life to start right now. Will you marry me?'

She leaned down to kiss him. 'Yes. We'll still make mistakes, Dylan. Neither of us is perfect. But we'll be in it together. We'll talk it through and we'll make it work.'

He got to his feet and kissed her lingeringly. 'You're right. And we don't have to be perfect. We just have to be ourselves. Together. I love you, Emmy.'

'I love you, too.' Her phone rang, and she smiled at him. 'I think that might be Syb. Our cue to go home.'

Home, Dylan thought. He was home at last. Because home was wherever Emmy was. 'To our baby. Because he is ours, Emmy. Just as you're mine.'

'And you're mine.'

He nodded. 'For now and forever'.

* * * * *

Mills & Boon® Large Print
January 2014

CHALLENGING DANTE
Lynne Graham

CAPTIVATED BY HER INNOCENCE
Kim Lawrence

LOST TO THE DESERT WARRIOR
Sarah Morgan

HIS UNEXPECTED LEGACY
Chantelle Shaw

NEVER SAY NO TO A CAFFARELLI
Melanie Milburne

HIS RING IS NOT ENOUGH
Maisey Yates

A REPUTATION TO UPHOLD
Victoria Parker

BOUND BY A BABY
Kate Hardy

IN THE LINE OF DUTY
Ami Weaver

PATCHWORK FAMILY IN THE OUTBACK
Soraya Lane

THE REBOUND GUY
Fiona Harper

1213 Rom LP

Mills & Boon® Large Print
February 2014

THE GREEK'S MARRIAGE BARGAIN
Sharon Kendrick

AN ENTICING DEBT TO PAY
Annie West

THE PLAYBOY OF PUERTO BANÚS
Carol Marinelli

MARRIAGE MADE OF SECRETS
Maya Blake

NEVER UNDERESTIMATE A CAFFARELLI
Melanie Milburne

THE DIVORCE PARTY
Jennifer Hayward

A HINT OF SCANDAL
Tara Pammi

SINGLE DAD'S CHRISTMAS MIRACLE
Susan Meier

SNOWBOUND WITH THE SOLDIER
Jennifer Faye

THE REDEMPTION OF RICO D'ANGELO
Michelle Douglas

BLAME IT ON THE CHAMPAGNE
Nina Harrington

0114 Rom LP

NEATH PORT TALBOT LIBRARY AND INFORMATION SERVICES							
1		25		49		73	
2	1/19	26		50		74	
3		27		51		75	
4		28		52		76	
5		29		53		77	
6		30		54		78	
7		31		55		79	
8		32		56		80	
9		33		57		81	
10		34		58		82	
11		35		59		83	
12		36		60		84	
13		37		61		85	
14		38		62		86	
15		39		63		87	
16		40		64		88	
17		41		65		89	
18		42		66		90	
19		43		67		91	
20		44		68		92	
21		45		69		COMMUNITY SERVICES	
22		46	4/20	70			
23		47		71		NPT/111	
24		48		72			